(*Reapers*) "....I got Reapers as a freebie ~~book and~~ didn't know what to expect. What an awesome surprise! Since reading this first book in the Druid Breeders series, I've bought the other available novellas (i only usually get the freebies) and am waiting with baited breath for the next addition, Seed! She's got me hook, line and sinker! I love the story, characters, descriptive sex scenes and the suspense! You won't be disappointed if you start the Druid Breeders adventure! I wish I was a Druid!!! ;)"
—*Skylar Griffin*

(*Bled*)"....I had no idea the books was so good. Druid Breeders series had everything I desired in books, alpha males, lots of action, steamy scene that would make your heart burst, die hard characters that I fell completely in love with, and a plot that completely kept me at the edge of my seat the whole way through the series."
—*Crystal R. "Crystal R."*

(*Harvest*) "....This is a series that keeps you guessing. In this installment, even more is going on with Rachel and Holly. More secrets are revealed and it has an ending with a twist. More about the Druid world is revealed and answers are given to the questions in the first two installments. This is a steamy steamy story that leaves you wanting more including a fan and glass of ice cold water"
—*Tabby*

THE
DRUID
SERIES

VOLUMES
1-3

MARATA EROS

THE DRUID SERIES
Volumes 1-3:
Reapers
Bled
Harvest

Copyright © 2011-2014 Marata Eros

ISBN-10: 1499265182
EAN-13: 9781499265187

THE DRUID SERIES 1

REAPERS

MARATA EROS

1

I looked at the clock, *yet again*...and knew that if my boss caught me I'd be toast. Safe in my cubicle, I swung my gaze away from the the dreaded time and looked for Michelle. She'd be hanging by the cooler, *which she was*.

Michelle caught me looking and lifted her chin up in greeting and grinned. She knew what I was about. It was all about getting out of here and doing something for ourselves. It had been a Long-Damn-Week and I was going to let my hair down and have some fun.

Michelle wrapped up her conversation with one of the petty chicks that lounged all day while we picked up the slack.

As Michelle walked toward me, I thought that maybe we wouldn't have to change: pencil skirts, thigh high stockings, stacked heels and blouses that yoked just where they should be to look sexy, nothing too much.

Michelle stood in front of me, tapping a foot. "Watching the time won't help it go faster."

"Yes, I know, but I feel like the day should have ended already."

"I've got an idea, let's go to Spinners tonight," she nearly squealed in delight. I wasn't feelin' the love on that place. It was always packed with a rough crowd and you had to beat the guys off with a bat.

Michelle saw my expression and started to wheedle immediately, "Listen, give it a half hour and if it's super-lame, we'll just bail and go somewhere else. Like that brewery place…what's it's name?"

"Talbot's," I replied absently.

She snapped her fingers. "That's it!"

"Listen," she leaned forward and our hair mingled together, "that new gal…with the red hair…"

"Molly?" I said, automatically looking around for her.

"Yeah," she waved her hand, dismissing the name. "She was talking about that piece of creepy news that's been circulating today."

I looked at her blankly.

"Oh for shit's sake, Rachel! Don't you pay attention to anything?"

"Not really," I said noncommittally. My life was beyond boring right now. I worked here, hung out with Michelle, worked out, read, fed my cat. I was dying for some Excitement. *Dying*. But the news wasn't going to deliver. Excitement…no way.

"You're hopeless! Anyway," she sounded the syllables out slowly, "there's been another killing. Another bleed-out."

That got my attention.

It had been almost a month since the first murder and they still hadn't found the killer.

Then there were the rapes.

Somehow, it was all connected. Men were killed and drained dry of their blood and if there were women with them, they were raped.

But none of the women could remember the attack or their attacker.

Our gazes locked. "So...they found another body. Two, actually." Michelle said ominously, waggling two fingers.

Great. Just when I thought we could flounce around for the weekend. Talk about a wet blanket.

"Maybe...we shouldn't go to Spinners then. I mean, if it's not safe."

"Eff-that, you're going! I just wanted to spread the gory gossip."

"That's kinda sick, you know."

Michelle nodded vigorously, she knew.

I sighed. There was no getting out of it once Michelle had her mind set. And, in my soul...if I didn't get a break from this job and do something out-of-body, I'd scream.

"I gotcha talked right into it, don't I?" Her eyes sparkled.

"I guess but, we need to be careful, especially now," I said in a conspirator's whisper.

"Hell, I'm more worried about the regular guys."

"Were the women…you know, was there blood… there?" I asked.

She spun back around, her skirt twirling a little with the motion. "That's the major weird thing, they had all been bitten, but still had their blood. Only a pint gone."

Well, wasn't that just *comforting*.

Michelle winked as she sauntered off, hips swaying. "Pick ya up at seven sharp."

She didn't wait for me to respond. Michelle knew she had me, hook, line and sinker.

I gathered up all my stuff, slipped my heels back on my feet and headed for the door.

Unfortunately, my dragon lady of a boss was blocking my way.

"Miss Collins, I see you're ready to leave." She looked at her behemoth of a wristwatch. "Two minutes after five." She raised a humongous unibrow at me and I stifled a giggle. It was hard to be pissed at her when she looked so ridiculous.

Almost.

"Yes. That's traditionally when the work day ends for us here, Ms. Hogan," I replied, thinking with mild irritation that Hogan had me by the short hairs. She knew I needed the job, she couldn't lambast me for leaving when the work day was through, technically. But…she liked to make me feel *diminished* for leaving so close to the chiming of the clock.

Hogan looked me over from head to toe, taking in my long black hair, so deep a black it had blue highlights in the right light. My eyes were a pale blue, I was shapely but not skinny, and on the tall side. I didn't consider myself a hot number but I held my own. Hogan, on the other hand looked like she was always trolling for a new bridge.

I had discreetly pressed my elbow into the elevator button and it dinged just as she opened her mouth to mention something else equally unimportant, her jowls swinging as she popped her mouth open then closed it again.

I felt my escape portal open at my back and walked backwards into its gaping mouth, never more glad to be out of mortar range of the enraged cow, aka my boss.

She glowered at me, starting to waddle forward and I blurted out, "Have a great weekend!" The door swept closed in front of me.

I did a mental forehead-wipe. Thank God I was out of there.

As the elevator descended I prepared myself for the onslaught of cold weather, my car would need at least five minutes to heat up. The days were long here in the north and heating my car in the underground parking garage was just part of what we did in Alaska.

The elevator doors hissed apart and the cold air swept into the tight space, momentarily stealing my breath. I huddled my full length coat around myself, silently wishing the car was already warm. I rushed out of the elevator's cocoon of heat, my heels making clicking sounds on the concrete as I made my way to my car. If you could call it that.

As I approached I knew my car stood out, it was a Smart Car and Michelle liked to tease and say it was a toaster that I drove, not a real car. I smiled, she had me there.

I fumbled with my keys, finally yanking my glove off with my teeth, groaning as the cold air assaulted my fingertips, making them instantly numb.

"Hey, Rachel,"

I dropped my keys on the ground, spinning, my hand to my heart.

It was Erik, a guy from work. My shoulders slumped in relief. He scared the shit out of me.

"Scare you?" he smiled.

I smiled back tentatively. He had really been pursuing me and I wasn't that interested. I couldn't put my finger on it exactly but there was just something *off* about him.

Erik approached me and I stiffened a little, but he bent over, jerking the keys off the ground and put a finger through the loop of my key fob and hung them off his finger in front of my nose.

I tried to snatch them and he yanked them just out of reach.

"Meet me for dinner," he stated, his eyes steady on my face, disconcerting.

"Ah...Michelle and I are going out tonight," I said, trying to distract him.

"Rain check?" he pressed, never stopping his eye contact. I was starting to get nervous.

Damn.

I resisted the supreme urge to look around, seeing if there was anyone else. But there wasn't. I could feel the absence of others. I sure wasn't short on woman's intuition. *Just another creepy service we offer*, I thought, getting the heebie-jeebies.

I closed my coat tighter around me and his eyes tracked the movement, a smile spreading on his face. "I'll let you go, I know you have plans." But his face told another tale. I didn't think he'd forget my rebuff anytime soon.

I held my hands out and I was happy to notice that they weren't shaking. He'd really put me in a creeped out mood and I wasn't happy about it.

He dropped the keys into my cupped hands and smiled again, tipping an imaginary hat.

I turned after his back was to me and stabbed the key into the lock, opening the door in one movement I slid behind the wheel, slapping the flat of my palm on the lock after it closed. I heard the simultaneous click in the silence of the car and let the breath out I didn't realize I'd been holding.

Holy-hell.

I turned on the car and stewed for the five minutes, all the while wishing I could have driven off.

That encounter with Erik had put a bad taste in my mouth. Like diet pop, but somehow worse.

I pulled out of the bowels of the building, the night as black as when the day started. I entered traffic and began the drive to my condo, almost in the heart of downtown.

I couldn't wait to be home.

I threw my lights on, and glancing right then left I was so startled that I almost let my foot off the brake into opposing traffic.

Erik sat behind the wheel of his car. He'd been sitting there the entire time...waiting for me.

I gunned it at the first hole in traffic that appeared. What a whacko!

I'd have to tell Michelle he was a nut-job. She'd have him cracked in no time.

I had my head thrown back and my lips parted, the last swipe of mascara almost perfect...there! I stood back and looked at my reflection: definitely not work attire. I was so glad I made the decision to not perk up the whole mess with just a new top. Michelle probably would have flogged me if I had anyway. She'd be dressed-to-kill (as usual). I needed to make an effort. Sometimes, I wondered why I bothered. Michelle would go, shine, get picked-up, bang some anonymous stud in the bathroom or wherever, and I would sip my drink wishing I could go home and curl up with a book. I sighed. That's okay. She was...my vicarious slutty friend. And I loved her.

I grabbed my vanilla body spray and squirted a last dab. If I ended up dancing a lot, I'd be glad I wore it. It was frigid outside but once we were inside Spinners, with all the bodies packed in there, it'd be a different story.

I heard the doorknob jiggle and caught sight of Michelle coming through the doorway looking delectable in her slut suit. She twirled for me so I could get the full effect.

"That should be illegal!" I nearly screamed. She had a micro-mini on that was two part: it cupped her ass and was barely legal (skimming the indecent exposure laws by a millimeter). It was hot pink, setting off her platinum hair to perfection. She "helped" the color of said hair, but not by a lot. Michelle was a rare thing up here in the frozen north and I was betting that it was her coloring that got her so much attention, and the boobs…and the outfits. And, and….

I smiled as she circled me like a shark, gauging my potential for Attracting the Opposite Sex.

"I don't know…is this the shortest skirt you have?" Her brows closed the distance between her eyes.

I self-consciously ran my hand over my short black skirt, it barely covered the lace of my thigh-highs…a gorgeous pair that I had splurged on from Italy.

"Yeah, I can't go much shorter without the lace tops showing."

Michelle gave me a blank look. "Seriously, that's part of the allure."

"Ah…no. I say let them guess. It *is* underwear after all."

"I say show it!" Michelle said.

"Mystery," I replied.

She threw her hand up. "Whatever, I give up. At least you did right by the top."

I had almost not worn it, it was a scorching crimson and showed off my raven hair, my eyes stranded like startled jewels in my pale face. It left my arms bare and was tucked inside the skirt.

Michelle allowed her glance to linger a moment longer on my outfit, then shook her head as we walked out. I gave a quick pet to Caesar the cat and waltzed out.

2

Spinners was packed as usual and we jockeyed for position, awkwardly elbowing everyone without trying to maim people. It was always this way.

I couldn't believe our luck! I spied a couple of bar stools and we raced over there to stake our claim before they were snatched up. We perched our butts on the stools, aimlessly looking around at the bodies packed together, dancing the night away. I noticed they had already opened all the windows, allowing the sub-twenty degree air in. It didn't matter, it felt like a balmy eighty where we sat.

The bartender got our drinks. I sipped on a Blue Hawaiian and Michelle had Sex on the Beach (of course). She swung her leg back and forth and I was getting a spot-on flash of bright red panties...and so were a bunch of guys, judging from the expression of the gaggle of hunks sitting across from us.

"So what happened with Erik?"

"Yeah!" I yelled to be heard over the din. "He did this weird thing with my keys…" and I told her the whole thing. Michelle leaned forward to catch everything because the noise was swallowing my words.

She leaned back against the bar, her elbows flung back and her wrists dangling off the edge, looking thoughtful. For Michelle that meant she was quiet for more than one minute.

Finally she said, "Yeah, you want to stay away from him. I hear he went out with some girl and date-raped her."

Perfect, I thought. That'd kinda been the vibe I was getting off him. Wasn't sure that confirmation was the greatest thing in this case, after all, I worked with the weirdo.

Wonderful.

I was momentarily distracted when two of the cute guys across the way sidled over to us. The one on the right was almost as blonde as Michelle but that's where the similarity ended. He was a head taller than her with brown eyes and a face that had seen acne in its youth. I guess he was ruggedly handsome. He spent time in the gym; it was in the set of his shoulders, the way he moved…like he had purpose.

Tonight his purpose was Michelle.

His eyes never left the foot that swung, traveling up to the apex of what the skirt almost showed. He looked like a dog ready to mount a bitch. It did something for her because her foot stopped swinging and she gave him the come hither look.

The night was Going According to Plan.

"Want to dance, cutie-pie?" she asked, batting her eyelashes. He all but panted while I rolled my eyes in my head. I just couldn't do it. It's not that I'd never had sex. Casual just wasn't a main entree. I dreamed that there was someone for me in my future. Someone that I could share something with. I felt almost like…almost like I was waiting.

Michelle argued there was plenty to be shared. She was into sharing.

Generous Michelle.

I watched her on the dance floor, plastered to Rugged, grinding for all she was worth, he was all over her and she was loving it.

I took my eyes off them and looked at the guy in front of me. He was way cuter than Rugged. He had the enigmatic *something* that made a girl want to get a little closer.

So I did.

"Do you want to dance?" he asked.

I nodded. He held out his hand, which was big I noticed. I tried not to think about how it would feel to have those hands roaming over my body but couldn't quite do it. He took me up against him and I molded against his torso. As those hands came to rest on the small of my back, the heat from them warmed me. He looked into my eyes and they held a promise of a fun night…if that's what I wanted. I didn't grind against him but I could feel that he was happy to be there. He smiled at me, knowing I was aware of his arousal.

He clutched me tighter and lowered his face next to mine and whispered, "Your friend's gone." Now he was kissing my neck.

Unease crept its way along my body. Usually Michelle gave me some kind of signal or something. I looked around for her trying not to feel frantic.

"Where did they go?" I semi-shouted at him.

"Outside!" He inclined his head in the direction of the door.

"You want to go find them?" he asked, his fingers already twining in mine.

I looked down at our clasped hands and that feeling of unease bloomed in me again. I couldn't shake it. I understood on some level that I was just getting residual anxiety from the strange encounter with Erik and letting that cloud my thinking. I wasn't going to take it out on this guy.

"Yeah, let's find them," I said decisively.

I should have listened to that voice inside my head.

3

The wind was up and tore at the light outfit I had chosen for dancing *inside*. It simply wasn't enough. But the guy, (Matt, he'd told me as we hurried out) had said he thought they'd be in the car.

"How much further?" I asked as I shivered in the light coat I'd slung on without a care before we left.

I cared now, I was freezing my half-naked ass off.

"Not much," he wrapped an arm around my shoulders as we walked and that helped.

Sure enough, another block of parked cars revealed a car that was running.

I could see a flash of pink in the car, but barely.

What was happening? It was Michelle but there were… others.

Other men.

My foreboding slammed back over me, washing away all tact. I went to wrench the car door open and Matt stopped me.

"They're busy."

"Ah duh, Einstein, I can see that. But I don't know if she was planning on being this busy," I said, seeing that there were at least two guys in there.

Matt put his hands up, as if to say, *hey, no problem, just sayin'.*

Irritating jerk.

Sighing, I tore open the door and was entirely unprepared for what I saw before me:

Michelle had Rugged behind her shoving his cock right up to her groin, the whole length of him digging in, sparing her nothing, his balls slapping her ass. The other guy, who I vaguely remembered sitting across the way from us, had his hand fisted in all that blonde hair and was pressing her face up and down on the shaft of his dick.

When the door opened, Rugged's eyes flew open and his gaze met mine. His body was pumping and working behind Michelle his hand reached over and slapped her ass and she moaned, her head working up and down the shaft of the prick she had in her mouth.

I didn't think she had planned on this and I yelled, "Michelle!"

She tried to take her head off the cock she was on but he shoved her back down and she gagged. "I'm gonna spray my cum you dumb bitch, keep sucking."

She squirmed to try and get away and Rugged held her hips, pounding into her harder. I backed away with my hand covering my mouth.

Michelle wasn't fooling around…she was getting raped.

I swung around to get help and Matt wrapped his arms around me. One of his big hands that I'd admired so much earlier covered my mouth so I couldn't scream.

Adrenaline slammed into me like a sheet of cold water.

Dragging me into the front seat of the car he threw me across and I bounced once, almost landing against the opposite door. Somewhere in the back of my mind I knew what was going to happen as Rugged said hoarsely, "God… I'm gonna cum in her snatch right now, oh God!"

The whole car rocked as he plunged his length into Michelle and the other guy torqued her head down on him and said, "Swallow it…that's it, *swallow it.* Ahhh…that's right," he groaned, throwing his head back, his lips slightly parted.

I started to fully panic then, scrambling across the seat, my skirt hiking around my hips as I struggled to reach the door.

Matt landed on top of me and all the air in my lungs went out in a rush. I couldn't breathe and was in a state of sheer panic, Matt was not the guy I had taken him for.

Neither were his friends.

I could hear Michelle sobbing softly and the rustle of her clothes as she tried to adjust everything.

Two heads and upper chests appeared over the top of the back seat as Matt's engorged arousal pressed along my inner thigh, trying to gain entrance, his pants long gone.

"You gotta a *live* one there," Guy X said.

"Not as 'live' as the bitch we just did," Rugged replied, laughing.

The sweet air of the car's interior entered in a rush, filling my lungs to capacity and I screamed for all I was worth, tearing something loose in the process. Matt's hand clamped over my mouth and I bit him, trying to meet my teeth together. He snatched his hand away and bellowed. I knew what was coming as I was pinned under him, his other hand came down with depressing speed and accuracy, slamming into my cheekbone, my head rocketing back against the door.

My head swam and his fingers dug at my panties while the other men watched....

Just when I thought there wasn't a hope in the world, the driver's side door was torn open, the hinges shrieking, then releasing in the process. The door was flung behind the figure that filled the opening.

I was seeing him upside down but the guys in the back seat summed it up, "What the fuck? Who the fuck are you?"

He was my savior...whoever he was.

Matt was backing off me in a hurry, leaving me to the stranger's mercy. With my head spinning all I saw was a strong jaw, black jeans, boots and a bad-ass leather zip-up. As he leaned down, the whiteness of his teeth gleamed in the interior dome light of the car, his nearly bald head had an inky wash of short black hair covering it, the shirt breaking open at the neck to reveal a tattoo that crawled up his neck.

He wasn't big on conversation, his hand snaking out in a lethal punch that terminated on Matt's nose. There was a sickening crunch and he backed up, howling. His bleeding hand with my teethmarks held what I was sure was a broken nose as he fell right outside the car on his ass.

The stranger looked down at me then and his eyes were a startling blue, not icy pale like mine. They were nearly white in a face that was pale, his lush mouth a deep scarlet slash. He looked me over carefully, but only a second or two as he was going to have to deal with Rugged and Guy X. Those two had gotten out of the car and I was too weak to even turn over and see things right side up. If he'd meant me harm, it would have happened.

At least that's what I told myself.

Rugged and Guy X faced him. "You could have had a piece of this action, if you'd asked nice."

The stranger looked briefly at Michelle who was trying to stop crying, the sobs turning to hitching hiccups. Then he spared a glance in my direction, taking in my clothes in disarray, my face starting to swell from the blow I'd received.

"They do not look as though it was the attention they wished for," the stranger responded.

I noticed that he was enormously big compared to the two men who had abused Michelle. And that was saying something because Matt had me by inches and I was five-eight.

Rugged said, "You talk funny."

"As do you," Stranger said.

Guy X circled around him, taking his measure as a male. "I think you need an ass-kicking. You've beat the shit

19

out of our car in the middle of fuckin' winter in this cold-ass place, ruined another piece of easy tail for me and my buds here. You gotta get what's comin' to ya."

Stranger looked at them as they rushed him at the same time. From my angle I saw everything upside down and in slow motion. Rugged came at him like a charging bear and Stranger swung his arm forward in a stiffened knife jab move and with the flat of the palm he landed it square in Rugged's nose. He stared blankly for a moment then fell like a box of rocks, his nose shattered. Guy X was a slow learner and grabbed him from behind and latched onto his wind pipe. Stranger grabbed the forearm which held him, crushing it before my eyes just using the one hand, while the other spun Guy X around to stare at him. He was howling, taking great lungfuls of air to bellow louder.

"Stop that noise," Stranger said.

And he did.

The stranger stared into the eyes of Guy X. "Tilt your head."

Guy X looked like he was in a fog, as if he was not in command of his mind. He cocked his head to the extreme left. The long, clean line of his neck was exposed under the street lamp, the artificial light casting a ghostly yellow on the flesh of his throat.

The stranger reared back like a snake and hissing, struck Guy X's neck. His teeth as he arced above Guy X's neck was something I would never forget:

They were fangs.

I was riveted. My presumed savior was not a man…he was something else. I had to get out of here. I tried to sit up and my head swam. I was woozy from the blow. The stranger had gathered Guy X in his arms and was taking great gulps from him but his eyes were pinned on me.

Time. To. Go.

I looked over the back seat and met Michelle's horrified eyes. Her mascara had made its way all over her face and I said, "Let's get out of here. *Right now.*"

I slid out of the car, one of my high heels falling off and was met by another stranger. This one had blonde hair and the same icy-blue eyes as the other.

They were busy tonight.

This one was all over Matt. He sucked at his neck while Matt made disconcerting mewling sounds underneath him. He lifted his mouth off Matt long enough to hiss at Michelle, which got us moving.

We backed away, both my shoes left on the sidewalk. They watched us but did not follow, taking the last of the men's blood. Their lives ebbed as we watched.

"What are they?" Michelle whispered.

"Ah…I think we've just been saved by those blood-killers."

"They…they raped the women…"

We looked at each other, dawning comprehension mirrored in our expressions.

We ran.

We ran until my lungs burned, the images of them sucking those guys lives away etched permanently in my brain. We were within sight of my car when we saw them leaning against it, one dark, the other light.

"Holy shit," Michelle stammered.

Yeah, that.

They came off the car at the same moment like perfectly choreographed twins. But it was the dark one that made my heart speed in my chest.

They came to stand before us. "We need to scrub them both. They have seen entirely too much," the blonde one said, his stare going from Michelle to me.

The dark one laid his icy gaze on me and I shivered. From what I didn't know but his gaze penetrated my bone and marrow.

"Holy shit," Michelle said again.

I seconded that.

Still I said nothing while they looked at us for a long moment. "No. The blonde one forgets. This one, no."

"Why, Cole?" the blonde stranger asked. "She is fair of face and figure, but there are many…"

"You cannot smell her?" Cole asked.

The blonde's head whipped around and his penetrating gaze was suddenly all for me; I backed away.

Finally, he shook his head. "All I smell is their fear. They smell like prey."

"Underneath that, Nathan."

One moment he was ten feet away and the next he had his arms around me and I screamed. Michelle started to run but faster than my eyes could track, the one named Cole had her in his arms, his hand covering her mouth and the fingers of those long hands feathered her temple. And I'd thought Matt's hand had been big...*my God*, his were palming her entire face.

Voices drifted down, the blonde's face was buried in my neck and I began to hyperventilate. Images flooded my mind of my would-be rapists not finishing what they started, distracted with death-by-blood loss.

"Be still," he said, his fangs bursting out of his mouth.

I thrashed around and he turned to Cole. "She will not follow my command."

"Will it so," Cole said.

He buried his nose in my neck, breathing my scent in, his fangs grazing the skin of my neck. Lifting his head he said, *"Breeder."*

"Yes."

"We must take her. There are so few left. This one is... she is rare."

A drunken group stepped out into our little mess and Michelle began hollering, "Help, help!"

A couple of the guys broke away from the pack and made their way over to us, Cole stood away from Michelle and the blonde released me slowly, like he didn't want to stop touching me.

As they approached the males, they looked into their eyes and each stranger said, "Leave this place." One of the men grabbed his temples with his hands, shaking his head like he couldn't release the clutches of something.

"That one has a strong mind," Nathan said.

"Some of the cattle do," Cole said.

Cattle.

I started to back away, subtly getting Michelle's attention. We were almost to the car when Cole's head whipped around. "You...will not leave."

Michelle began hollering again but the men walked away. The one who shook his head cast a final glance behind him. As we watched he massaged his temple, continuing to walk away.

They retraced their steps toward us and my heart sank. We could not outrun something we couldn't see move, something that crushed a man's face with one swipe, disintegrated an arm with a grip strong enough to pulverize bone. As they drew nearer, their fangs stood out of their mouths, barbed points ready to pierce our flesh.

Michelle latched on to my hand and I prepared myself for the worst.

"You cannot thirst."

"No, but the blonde one's fear is an aphrodisiac," Nathan said.

"Yes, but think on this Nathan: has she not already been degraded enough by the human scum we dispatched?" Cole said.

"Yes," Nathan ground out. "You speak true."

"Then scrub her and we take the female breeder."

Nathan approached Michelle and she started to wail, her screams broken only by her next breath.

The blonde was suddenly in front of her. Squeezing her throat lightly, he cut off her screaming and the sudden silence filled the parking area. The snow was falling softly around us, some of the flakes catching in my eye-lashes. Nathan stared deeply into Michelle's eyes. Finally he moved away and she stood there, blank faced, in a zom-bie-like stupor.

"What did you do to her?" I whispered.

"Something we cannot do for you," Cole remarked.

I backed away and they tracked me. "I am not going with you," I said, proud that my voice only shook a little.

"We understand your fear, but you will come with us. How do you humans put it? It is *non-negotiable*."

"You don't understand anything! You two...whatever-you-are, sucked our attacker's blood. They died and *now* you're calling me some kind of 'breeder'. No offense, but it's not looking too good on my end."

My eyes bounced from one to the other of them. I couldn't follow their movements, just when I thought I had one in my sights they moved so fast they were both suddenly one foot away from me, each holding an arm. I opened my mouth to scream and Cole put his mouth on mine, stifling it. His kiss blossomed and spread to the center of me, making my panties instantly moisten. I'd never had a reaction like this in my life.

Of course, I'd always made out with human men.

My fear was in my throat but my biology was never touched by it. I couldn't move my arms but as my mouth moved against his, he released my arm and I wound it around his neck, pressing his lips harder against mine and he groaned and pulled me against him. My mind played tug-of-war, my intellect was screaming that he was some creature of the night. He'd killed two men before my eyes but my center bloomed for him; heat stretching and spreading from between my legs. My nipples hardened and he reached behind me, placing his hands under my thighs. Never breaking from the kiss, he lifted me up and I wound my legs around his waist.

"She is so eager," Nathan said, releasing my other arm. He circled us, grabbing a piece of my hair and flicking it behind my shoulder.

That broke through the heat of the moment and my intellect slammed back into place. I broke away and shoved at his chest with my hands. He let me slide down his body and when my feet hit the pavement, the cold moved up my legs, freezing that searing heat before it progressed.

I gave Nathan a dirty look, noticing Michelle still stood there in the same position, gooseflesh covering her arms, her teeth chattering.

"I don't know what you are, or why this is happening but I just want you to go…now. I will get my friend and I home without any help from you." I folded my arms across my chest.

"Your body speaks for what you want. It speaks for what you are."

"Oh?" I arched my eyebrow. "What is it that *I* am?"

"It is what is in your blood, you are of Druid blood. They are the only humans that may breed with us."

Druid? What the hell was that?

Okay, next question:

"What are you?"

They looked at each other. "We are Vampire, *witch*," Cole said as if that should have been obvious.

Witch? Had the conversation devolved to name-calling at two a.m.?

"Do you know of your people?"

I couldn't believe I was standing out here in twenty degree weather talking to a couple of guys claiming to be vampires. I felt incredibly stupid to have kissed the one… *Cole.*

"Ah, no. I'm adopted. Okay, while all this is interesting, it's time to go."

I turned to Michelle, who had a spot of drool coming out of her mouth. God, what did they do to her? I walked over to her, grabbing a limp arm and started dragging her to my car.

Suddenly, they stood in front of me.

"Would you stop doing that!" I said, fear choking me.

A smile spread over Cole's face. "Doing what?" His fangs were smaller now that he wasn't trying to French me.

Sirens began in the distance and we all looked in their direction.

"The human police," Nathan said.

"Yes."

"Another time, *breeder*," Cole said. He licked his finger and touched it on my forehead. "I mark you for another time, very soon."

They disappeared into thin air and I was left with Michelle, the approaching cops, and a pulsing core that wept for the vampire that was now gone.

4

My eyes felt like they had crushed glass in them but I wasn't going to bed any time soon. These assholes had made me repeat the same answers to the same shit about two hundred times. I was getting pissed. Poor Michelle was curled up, sleeping on the couch, a rape kit finished and being processed.

"Okay, Miss Collins, I want to ask you one more time," the detective ran slim hands through his hair, making it whack out in all different directions. Its honey-colored goodness would have been fun to look at had I not been at the Anchorage Police Station at going on four-oh-hell in the morning.

"You claim your friend," and he threw a look at Michelle, who was a small mound under the gunmetal gray blanket they'd thrown over her on the lumpy precinct couch, "was attacked." He looked down at his notepad, scrolling down with his finger until he found the detail he was looking for, "...by two men, claiming to be vampires.

That, inadvertently," he made airquotes here, "saved you from the attackers."

I wanted to punch him in the snout, he was just *that* condescending.

I was so done here. "Listen…Detective…"

"Jewel, Christopher Jewel."

Fine. "Anyway, my friend just got a *fun* rape kit done, and you have three bodies without any blood…right?"

He tapped his pen on his notepad. "Actually, we have evidence that suggests there was an incident at that location, but there has not been any bodies recovered."

Wow…the vampires had done away with the evidence. My heart sped thinking about how fast they'd had to been to go back to the scene and get rid of three men before the police got there.

"And the vampire story…" he looked at me like, *you really expect me to believe this?*

"That's what they told me," I replied.

"That is a myth, there are no such thing as vampires. However, I know from the minute that you came in here I have not been able to get touching you out of my mind." His eyes stared into mine and I got up so quickly from the chair it fell over with an echoing clatter of metal against tiled linoleum.

He walked over to me as if he was in a fugue. "You smell," and he leaned in as I leaned away, "very good."

Okay, now things were getting weird. Mr. Professional Cop was coming on to me in the middle of the police station when he should be getting my statement.

"It says here that, 'he was kissing me, then heard the police sirens and he and the other vampire left'," he resumed his questioning.

I nodded. Maybe he'd get off all the personal weirdness then. I covertly looked around in the hopes of spotting another cop. There was only Michelle on the couch and a lone secretary waaayyyy down the hall.

Shit.

As if on cue, he walked over to Michelle. "She smells fuckable too," he said and with that, he whipped off the cover and spread her legs.

She stirred in her sleep when I yelled, "Hey!" This couldn't be happening. Where was everyone? What-the-hell?

What the blue fuck was wrong with him?

But he'd already put a finger inside her, and started pumping it back and forth. "Yeah, she's still really lubed up from all that cum that got dumped in there."

I ran over there and shoved him and he turned, my friend's crotch spread to the world. He backhanded me and I spilled on the floor as he all but ran over to the door, closing it and locking it in place. My face stung unmercifully having just been hit in the same spot a couple of hours before.

It felt like days.

Where the hell were all the other cops?

I tried to scramble to my feet but he tackled me, tearing at my skirt and ripping down my panties. I responded with a knee to the crotch, my jaw on fire.

As if from a distance, I heard a crash and glass shattered behind me, falling like crystal rain all around us, my arms shielding my face.

I didn't open my eyes as Detective Jewel was torn off me. I became aware of the fact that there wasn't any more noise and cold air was rushing in and…I had no clothes on.

I closed my legs all the way and threw my hands down to cover the apex of my thighs.

I opened my eyes and there were Nathan and Cole, the vampires were back.

"Has she been…violated?" Nathan asked.

Cole bent down, putting his nose right above my crotch and I flinched, he laughed. He shook his head. "No, there is no human taint upon her."

He jerked his head in the direction of the secretary and said, "Take care of the human female and all that you encounter in the interim."

Nathan nodded and sped down the hall, a blur of gray, the black softened by the motion of his body.

Cole swung his gaze back to me. "Are you alright?"

I nodded stiffly, his voice was like velvet gravel and I became aroused again. I was instantly furious with myself. I had just about been raped by a police officer for shit's sake and here I was: ready-to-hump a stranger that wasn't even human. I started shaking from shock and cold.

Perfect.

"I'm fine," I said, getting up unsteadily and searching for my skirt without a shred of dignity. Difficult to have *any* when you were wearing a top, thigh-highs and nothing else.

Cole-the-vampire held out my skirt, which dangled from a finger but the panties were beyond repair. I grabbed it and threw it on, hopping twice to get it zipped up. As I'd been getting the skirt on Cole stared at my body, his eyes missing nothing. I was still flushed by the scrutiny and feeling vulnerable. There was no place that was safe. The police station was not safe, *obviously*, and the dangerous vampires were back. Their motivations were suspect.

Nathan burst back into the grim interrogation room and nodded at Cole. "It is done."

Cole looked at me. "Time to go."

"No," I said, backing away.

"It is not safe for you here. The human males smell us on you...*on her*." He gave a dismissive glance at Michelle. "They will try to take you by force."

"What does that have to do with anything?"

Nathan shrugged. "They are little more than the basest animals. They smell vampire pheromone and it causes a territorial urge that they can't intellectualize away."

"They wish to mate with any female that comes into close contact with one of our kind. It is primal. They think if *they* can impregnate *you*, then we obviously...cannot."

Made a warped kind of sense. I had a sudden thought. "But Michelle isn't a 'breeder'."

Cole smiled, turning to Nathan. "I told you the Druids were superior. It is more than just bloodline. It is many things."

Nathan grunted. He didn't sound convinced.

They looked at me and I stared back. Finally, I shook my head. "I'm sorry, I don't know you and you're obviously dangerous…I have a life here," I said by way of explanation.

"We know of your life, Witch," Cole said.

"It's Rachel."

"Rachel," his voice caressed each syllable and I was *so* into that sound, like spoken velvet caressing things down low in my body. I had to shake my head to get rid of the urge to undress right there.

Nathan laughed. "She is ready for you, Cole."

"Yes."

That was so unflattering. What? Could they smell my arousal?

Nathan nodded, interpreting my expression. "We know when you are ripe, female. We must. How many breeders are in existence for us?"

"Too few," Cole responded.

Jewel was coming to his senses. He swung his head from side to side, trying to clear it. He got up from all fours and started to come for me and Cole turned to him. "Not her," baring his fangs with a hiss.

Jewel looked bewildered but only for a moment, then his gaze fixed on Michelle and he walked toward her.

"No!" I yelled. "He can't rape her!"

But Cole and Nathan shook their heads, holding me back from saving my friend.

"We need him to be distracted from taking you. He will not remember. He will fuck the human female and they will be caught up in dealing with him and...her."

I watched in muted horror as Jewell dropped his pants, inserted a finger inside her and with a satisfied nod, he pushed his shaft in deeply, working it in and out, never even glancing our way. Michelle's eyes flew open and she started to holler and Nathan stalked over to her, looking deeply in her eyes he said, "You're coming."

Michelle began to scream in a whole different way, her core grabbing onto Jewel's cock as he ground it into her. He sped his pace as we all watched, tears silently streaming down my face. My friend used a pawn on the chessboard of everyone else. As Jewell finished up, his balls slapping her ass, he groaned, "Ah, yeah..." and with several quick thrusts, he collapsed on top of her.

"I can't do this," I said, backing away from everyone. I couldn't help Michelle as Jewel flipped her over on her stomach.

"What's he doing?" I nearly yelled.

"Her ass, I think," Nathan said casually.

I ran then.

I ran down the hall, past people that stood in a stupor and didn't see me. I rushed outside in a ripped skirt, heels and a torn blouse moving swiftly to my right, heading straight for the first building I could see.

I could get help, I thought.

Suddenly, a large hand clamped on my shoulder and whirled me around.

It was Cole. "You *will* come with us."

He put a bag over my head and Nathan tied my wrists together. A feeling of weightlessness overcame me, causing me to feel at once heavy and light. My vision receded to a small point of light. Then...even that went black and I knew no more.

5

I cracked my eyelids open and looked around at where I was, disoriented and flushed, my first vision was of a stone ceiling.

Where was I?

Shit! Remembering the last twenty-four hours made my head ache. The memories came crashing down on me like rain on a tin roof.

I sat up slowly. My wrists were now unbound and the bag that had covered my head lay on top of a thick and solid wood bureau that sat underneath a leaded window, diamonds fracturing the light as it came through the glass.

I stood up on feet without heels, my skirt a tangled mess and walked over to the window. I looked through the molded panes. The warped glass offered a view of extensive grounds that rolled off into the distance, covered by a glittering white carpet of snow. Spruce trees danced in the wind at the perimeter of the compound.

Because that was what this was, I was sure, seeing the outline of a great stone wall that followed the forest border. I turned, taking in the surroundings of my room. Aside from the solitary window, there was a bed, the dresser and a large mirror. It was so large it took up a third of the wall. *That was strange*, I thought, approaching it.

I stood in front of the mirror, gazing at my reflection and noticed the crimson blouse was worse-for-wear, the black skirt ruined, the thigh-highs from Italy, torn. But it was my face that looked different; absolutely pale like alabaster. Purple smudges underneath my blue eyes like bruises, my lips a deep pink in a sea of pale flesh. I shuddered, looking down at where my watch usually was...it had vanished. My disquiet deepened, I didn't know what day it was, what time it was and my stomach ached from the need to eat.

I walked back over to the bed and sat down, dejected.

I guess I had more to worry about than losing my crummy cubicle job. Like, *where the blue hell was I*? Was I going to live? Was this the rest of my life...a life where I was a "breeder?" I didn't even know if I wanted children. I'd never dated anyone I could imagine that life with.

It sure wasn't a vampire. That whole concept didn't compute. And what about all that talk of being of Druid blood? Being a witch. I wasn't anything...really. My adopted family had been atheists and I'd just swung along in their non-religious ocean. I sighed.

Answers, I needed answers.

Just then, the thick wood door surged open and I leaped up, instantly finding the wall with the back of my hand.

It was Nathan, the vampire that had let Detective Jewel abuse Michelle. He looked different in this context: the context of me being alone in a bedroom with him.

I assessed him as a male, so different than Cole but eerily the same. His icy-blue eyes, exactly the same color of Cole's, gleamed underneath a strong brow with golden blond hair that was so pale it was almost white. His shoulders were broad and tapered to a trim waist. He was an enormous man, at least six foot four. Even so, Cole was even taller.

My eyes narrowed; I was pissed at him. He'd left my friend with the creeper-cop and now I was here against my will. They'd have a fight on their hands. I wasn't just going to roll over and let them scratch my belly.

He moved forward and I shrunk against the wall. "Stay over there, freak," I said.

He smiled, never pausing his strides, coming to stand an uncomfortable foot or so away from me. It would have been easier to touch me but he hovered, not committing to tactile just yet.

"We are at the top of the food chain, Witch. Humans live by our sufferance alone."

I nodded, *right*. He was obviously insane.

"Doesn't look like you're keeping things under wraps too well. Judging by the psychos that are running around raping and bleeding out everyone of late." I folded my arms across my chest, going for nonchalant know-it-all.

His eyes bored into mine. "Those are *rogue* Vampire. We were trailing them when we came upon you and the human female."

"Excuse me! I am a human female!"

"Not exactly," Nathan said, leaning in to smell me. His hands were on either side of my head, his nose hovering above my neck. I ducked, moving under his arms and he was right in front of me again, moving so fast I hadn't see him and I yelped. He hissed in response, his fangs punching out of his mouth, the tips glistening in the low light of the room.

My heart sped, I tried to make myself smaller against the wall but I was effectively trapped and at his mercy. That just pissed me off more, my anger eclipsing my fear.

"Nathan!" a voice said from the door.

He leaned back from me slowly and I moved into the corner and looked at who had spoken.

It was Cole, looking like he had the prior night, all-black and menace.

He looked especially menacing right now, hadn't even bothered to look in my direction, his eyes were all for Nathan. And those eyes were boiling with rage.

"You are cognizant of the rules, stay away from her."

"You just want to be first with her."

They stared at each other for a swollen moment. My heart was in my throat. Here were a couple of vampires, casually discussing who would have sex with me first. Like I was a commodity.

Swell.

"Hey boys," I waved my hand so they'd notice me in the corner.

"Maybe I don't want either one of you, hmm?" I smiled.

Cole moved so fast it was that blur of gray again and I steeled myself. I kept chanting in my mind that there'd been ample opportunity to kill me if that had been their intent. But having six-foot five of fast and pissed male *vampire* pressed up against my body was a whole different thing.

My pulse raced in fear as my body responded in anger.

He dragged a finger down the side of my neck, leaving a burning trail of heat and stopped at the thrumming and jumping pulse in the hollow of it. "I think you speak prematurely, Witch."

"It's Rachel, freak."

He snatched his hand away. "We are not freaks. We are superior to humans in every way."

I shoved him with both hands but he was like an immoveable wall. "Good, then you should have no trouble letting me go since I am an *inferior human*."

I was all fake bravado but maybe that'd work.

It didn't. He pulled me into his arms and I struggled to get away as he crushed his mouth to mine. Those fangs of his pierced the tender inside of my mouth and a few drops of blood filled my mouth from the force of his kiss.

The scent of my blood bloomed in the room and suddenly Nathan was there, ripping Cole off me. They turned on each other hissing as Cole shoved me behind him.

Unbelievable, I thought, licking my lip and tasting copper.

Nathan watched my tongue flick over the small wound Cole had made like a starving man.

Starving vampire.

Cole forgotten, Nathan lunged for me and Cole barreled into him, both of them crashing into the stone wall.

More vampires filled the room, their eyes taking in the scene before them, their stares falling on me. I went back into the corner and their eyes tracked me like prey.

Holy-hell. This was looking bad. No, check that…it was bad.

"Who has bled her?" the leader asked, a huge signet type ring glinting on his middle finger; a swollen ruby that reflected their precious blood.

His hand covered his nose and he breathed out of his mouth, as did the others.

Wasn't this special?

His gaze watched me with a hunger that was alive. He actually took a step backward. "Cole, Nathan!" he barked.

They broke apart, both faces swollen from abusing each other. Their chests heaved from exertion.

The Leader said, "You understand better now, no?"

Cole looked at him and nodded. "It was not I that transgressed, it was Nathan, Alexander."

Alexander looked at Nathan. "You came here to see her…*alone.*"

"Yes," he spit a wad of blood onto the floor. They bled red, just like humans, I noticed a trifle smug.

Alexander's eyes narrowed on Nathan. "You bled her as well."

Nathan looked at Cole. "The witch enticed him."

I huffed and they looked at me. "Ah, excuse me, Superior Vampires, but I am *not* wanting your twisted attention, thanks. Just so we're clear."

Alexander's dead glacier eyes looked into mine. "You will."

I shrugged, let him think what he wanted. I was desperate to give him the middle finger salute but held back. I think I may have caused enough trouble as it was.

For now.

One of the other vampires said to him, his stare never leaving me, "She is bold with her words, this one. How much Druid blood does she have?"

Cole looked shamed but answered, "Much."

Alexander swung his head to Cole. "A pureblood?"

Cole shrugged. "I would not know for certain, but I have not tasted purer than hers."

Wonderful. As fun as all this was, "Here's the thing," they all looked at me again. Six identical crystalline blue eyes, their weighty stares were disconcerting as hell. "I have a life. That I want to go back to. I am not a witch…I don't know about this 'blood thing'. You're holding me against my will. I promise…I won't tell the, ah…*humans* about you. Just let me go." As I said that my eyes swung instinctively to Cole who shook his head slightly.

No dice.

"We cannot release you. Even if you had just an distant Druid relative, you would still be a viable breeder. Now," he swung his palms out away from his sides, "a pureblood would mean much more."

Alexander moved slowly to me. I think he was trying to keep me calm, but his slow approach was almost worse.

My palms grew damp and I wiped them on the wrinkled skirt.

"Let me taste you, Witch."

I shook my head, his face inches from mine.

His eyes stared deeply into mine and I felt him pushing at me but it sloughed off like water off a duck's back. The mental ability that they used on others was not having the slightest effect.

"I don't have to ask you. Cole?" he directed at Cole without turning from me.

"Yes?"

"She does not respond to compulsion," he stated.

"No."

"Definitely a pure parent at least." He leaned closer, sniffing me.

His fangs elongated slowly.

I shrank away, none of the desire I'd had for Cole with this one. He only filled me with fear as he prepared to strike the vulnerable flesh of my neck.

I threw my hand into his face and it slowed him for a moment and I yelped, retreating. He lunged for me, spittle hanging out of his mouth, a ravenous expression covering his face. When Cole appeared out of nowhere he hissed at Alexander his body crouched in front of me. I stifled a whimper but he heard it, his body stiffening.

"Are you bonding with this breeder, Cole?"

"No, but you scare her to taste her. We are trained to *not* harm the breeders. *Think,* Alexander, if she had been stumbled upon by the *rogue.* We are not savages, we are Vampire."

Alexander straightened.

He glared at Cole, his eyes flicking to me then back to him. "You are right, I have lost myself. It has been some time since I have been exposed to...a pure breeder." His gaze bored into mine.

"She goes nowhere. Two of you visit her together, no exceptions. There is time yet to ascertain the purity of her blood. But mark my words, it will be soon."

He looked at me one last time then left, taking his two "guards" with him.

Cole and Nathan looked at me.

Finally Cole said, "We will send a female to help you clean up and get some clothing for you. Tomorrow there will be a ceremony and your life here amongst us will begin."

With that, he gave me a final stare and they left.

Great.

I was locked in a house with a bunch of gang-rapists whose primary goal was to get me pregnant.

Every girl's dream.

6

I waited in my austere room for this elusive "female" that would give me clothes.

I didn't sit on my ass, I paced.

I spent an inordinate amount of time beside my window gazing out at the crystallized brightness, the white glancing of the sun casting diamonds on the ground.

A soft knock sounded and a woman entered, her belly swollen. I took in her simple attire of flowing tunic and linen pants, simple flats completed the look. Something about her made my soul clench, like a bell had been rung that only I could hear.

She smiled at me, she felt it too.

"You are Druid," she said as statement. Her hair was as black as my own, flowing about her waist like silken water.

"I...I don't know," I stammered, feeling very unbalanced, surreal.

"I am Eve." She came forward with her hand out and I shook it, rapidly stepping back.

Eve put some things down on the end of the bed and brought a key out of her pocket. It gleamed like melted butter in the low light of the room.

"I was told that you needed to clean up…"

"I don't want to be here," I said, frustrated. She was human, surely she could understand it.

"They will not let you go. You must understand how rare you are. How rare we all are." She held out her hands in supplication.

"Do you know your kin?" Eve asked.

I shook my head. "I was adopted…I didn't know that I was anything but single white female, age twenty-eight." I shrugged.

Eve smiled and it broke the ice. "Let's get you in a bath and some fresh things. You will feel much better after you are clean. And," her hazel eyes met mine, "they sent me for a reason. They wish for you to feel more at ease."

Eve spoke very strangely, I could feel my face scrunch up and I asked, "Are you…how old are you?" I looked at her swollen stomach and felt a heat rise on my cheeks.

"Come," she held out her hand and I took it as we walked into the bathroom together where she closed the door softly behind us.

Like the rest of the structure, the bathroom was all clean, old-fashioned lines with a huge claw-foot tub that stood in the center atop a marble platform.

Eve cranked open the taps and feeling the water temperature she nodded to herself, laying the towels beside the tub on a small wooden stool of sorts and turned to me. The pipes moaning in the bathroom were the only sound.

"You have met Cole, Alexander and…?" She hesitated.

"Nathan," I filled in reluctantly.

"You understand they do not think as human males do?"

I nodded, I was fully getting that.

I stripped in front of Eve, any self-consciousness gone before my desire to get the soiled and ruined clothing off me. She watched me silently, her eyes roving my body and she nodded. "You are not modest?"

I shook my head and shrugged. "Not in front of other women. In front of *them*, I wouldn't feel real comfortable taking my clothes off."

She laughed as I put a toe in the water. Inch-by-inch I sunk down into the scented and steaming bath water, the stress and fright of the last twenty-four hours melting away and I sighed in contentment. Human again, if only for the moment.

Then Eve spoke and it slid back into me again.

"Two of the vampire claim me as mate," she said in that matter-of-fact way of hers, her hand automatically going to her belly.

My shoulders were just covered with water as she handed me the soap and the shampoo and I suddenly thought of Michelle and my face beat with shame, hot and flushed and Eve noticed.

"What troubles you?"

Geez, was she really asking that? Let me see, my best friend was being raped and I left her for there. My cat doesn't have anyone there to take care of him.

My job.

My job! I think it was safe to say that would be gone as well and I sighed.

I turned the tables on her. "Please answer some questions I have for you. If you really want me to feel better."

Eve waited, all calm and unflappable.

"How old are you?"

"I am one hundred five," she answered with a straight face.

"Are you shitting me?" I asked without grace.

Eve's face took on a puzzled frown.

She didn't understand me.

I rephrased, "Are you joking? I mean, that's not possible." I held out my hand indicating her obvious youth and pregnancy.

She smiled. "I am Druid and I have been with the vampires since the 1930s. We do not age when we are in their care."

Do not age. I wasn't sure that was such a hot benefit. Who said living forever was so great?

She reached out and tenderly put a strand of my hair behind my ear, the wetness of it clinging to the back of my neck.

"How much," I stumbled over the next word, "Druid blood do you have?"

She shook her head. "Enough to breed," she lifted a shoulder in a partial shrug, "maybe one-eighth or thereabouts."

"How can they know what you are, how much? And do you just become, what? A baby-maker?"

Eve blushed and I immediately regretted all my rude questions. But, I was the kidnapped party here and even though it was not her fault directly, I had no one else to pose these questions to. I was deeply unhinged that I was so attracted to the one vampire, Cole.

I shouldn't have been.

"We may only have one baby per decade and if we are quite fortunate, it will be a Druid female. Female vampires are usually sterile," she held up a finger, "but not always, and of course, male vampires are born to us."

God, the breast-feeding must be hell, I shuddered. Yuk. She saw my face and asked, "What?"

"I was thinking about feeding the baby...?" I let that loaded question hover like a pink elephant in the room and Eve laughed.

"The vampire infants have retractable fangs, my dear." Wonderful.

"Would you help me escape this place?" I asked. I was *not* interested in being sequestered in this weird-ass castle or whatever it was.

She shook her head. "You don't understand. They will *never* let you go with their suspicions of your pureblood. Why, you could be mated to a vampire, fought over, have twins; pure Druid children. Male Druid children can impregnate the female vampires. You are a precious jewel to them, Rachel."

I was getting out of here. Even my boring cubicle job was sounding better. I'd play along and find my cell, call Michelle and figure out my future.

I smiled, feeling it like plastic on my face and Eve's brows came together in a pretty frown.

"I guess I'll make the best of it," I said with false cheer and finished my grooming, shaving, scrubbing, and washing my long hair three times. I felt like I'd never get clean after what I'd been through.

Thoughts of my friend and my life were a dismal pulse beating in my brain.

7

I slid into the clothes that had been provided and they were nothing like what Eve had been wearing. For one thing, there were no tags. I slid on a thinly made, silk skirt with a hidden zipper in the back and low-heeled sandals, it was winter but the place was kept quite warm so my legs were left bare. Finally, a deep royal blue sleeveless shirt finished the ensemble. Eve had given me lingerie that seemed contrary to the plain yet elegant clothing I'd been given; crimson lace boy panties and bra set. The bra hugged my breasts like lace skin, molding and pushing them up to what felt like my neck level. Once the blouse was on, my breasts floated at the top of the blue like creamy flesh balloons.

I'd keep the bra when I got out of here I thought with a smirk.

I found my cell after Eve left with a suspicious glance over her shoulder and I heard the bolt slide into place from the outside. I would have to leave this room first, then scope out possible portals of escape.

The hopelessness of my situation did not escape me. I was with a bunch of predators, bent on having me and keeping me...virtually forever. But I wasn't one to give up.

I snapped up my cell and the bar for service was at one. And so was my charge.

Quickly I speed-texted Michelle, thinking...*respond, respond, respond.*

The envelope lit up on my cell and I punched the screen and Michelle's text appeared.

Where the hell are you? You dumbass, the cops have been crawling all over your apartment looking for you! And! They found the bodies of the guys that attacked me...

I sent back this message:

I've been taken by the freak-vampires and am trying to figure out an escape plan.

I glanced around. Went to the window, looked outside. I had no idea where I was. Wherever it was, the woods didn't narrow things down.

Somewhere rural I thought, despairing.

Well...I am doing cat-sitting right now. Do you know where you're at? Are you okay?

Yeah, I'm okay. Are you…alright? Has the cop been arrested? I texted.

Why? What cop? Michelle texted back.

She didn't know? I thought.

The one that was busy raping you in the interrogation room…

I think you're confused, Rach. I mean, the two jerks at Spinners were the ones that raped me. The cop is the one that ordered the rape kit and drove me home.

Scrubbed.

The vampires had erased her memory. As far as Michelle knew, the rapists were dead and in the ground now. Never to do a repeat performance.

The bolt slid back and Nathan and Cole strode in the room, Cole's eyes honed in on the cell open and lit in my hand.

He was upon me in an instant, the cell swept against the wall and shattered before I knew my hand was empty.

Nathan held both my wrists together in a grip that was achingly tight, just shy of crushing and I moaned against my will, it hurt that much.

Cole turned and said, "Release her fool, she is fragile."

Nathan did, smiling and Cole frowned at him.

I fought the urge to rub my wrists as Nathan's eyes roved over my body. "Mouthwatering," he said. "Her scent permeates the air."

Cole nodded. "It does," he said, his breath quickening.

They approached me slowly and I backed up into the corner of the room, thinking that was becoming a familiar theme for me.

My body responded to their closeness and my knees grew weak as Cole leaned into my neck, his fangs punching out with a snapping, meaty sound and I shuddered, my desire and fear mingling in exquisite torture.

Nathan moved in on the other side, wrapping his muscular arm around my waist and holding me against him. Cole began to kiss my neck and simultaneously graze those fangs along my jawline. Nathan wrapped a hand in my hair and exposed my neck in a long, clean line and my breath came in ragged gulps, my core getting wet for invasion, thoughts of my escape dimming as my desire for the vampires overcame my sense.

"I will taste you now, Witch. And you will let me," Cole said, his hot breath warming my slender throat, the pulse beating wildly beneath his mouth.

Something fundamental inside me screamed *no* even as my arms drew him into my body and he struck, his fangs sinking into my throat, latching on.

It was the worst pain of my life. I began to struggle and Nathan held me still, my body bucking as Cole drank my blood, his arousal against my belly while his fangs pierced my flesh.

As my head became light, Cole pulled back, licking the wounds at my throat and I slid down the front of Nathan's body, dizzy.

Cole caught me easily, carrying me to the bed where they lay me on it.

"She is pure. Both parents, Druid," Cole said as I stared up at him dreamily.

"She will not fight us now," Nathan said, his eyes on my legs, breasts, all of me.

"Alexander will punish us for having her before the ceremony."

Cole looked at Nathan. "He need not know."

A silent glance passed between the two vampires and I felt the weight of their stare like licking heat on my body.

The blood loss had made me feel drunk, but the feeding at my throat had awakened something primal in me. I felt desire for Cole spread like a flower opening deep inside my body.

He must have sensed something because he looked down at me.

"I cannot, it is akin to rape. She is in blood-languor. She would have sex with any one of us. And," Cole said, stroking the flat of his palm over one of my nipples until it hardened, "Alexander would find what vampire would be the most fertile with her."

Nathan said, "Fine, but we must see if we can give her something for the gift of her blood."

A slow smile spread over Cole's face and I lay there as they discussed having sex with me and found I couldn't work up to a point of indignation. What was wrong with me? My throat throbbed and my core moistened in anticipation for their attention.

Slowly, Cole put his large hands at the hem of the skirt and raised it inch by slow inch until it was exposing the beautiful crimson panties. His blunt fingertip slowly teased the inside of the lace edge against my vulnerable opening, not reaching inside, just stroking the side of the panty. I moaned and my legs began to part of their own volition. I was deeply embarrassed, but too aroused to care.

Cole gave a masculine chuckle and inserted the one finger that had ridden the edge of the lace into me and was greeted by my slickness and he groaned. "She is so ready," he murmured.

His hand began to work a rhythm and my hips squirmed to meet it. Nathan had unbuttoned my blouse and was rolling my nipples in between his fingers as Cole moved a finger in and out of me in a slow and delicious pull.

I looked up at his glacial eyes, watching him down the long line of my body as my skirt sat bunched around my waist and his hand was busy inside me.

I was building toward a shattering orgasm when he surprised me out of my languid stupor by pressing his mouth against my clit, flicking it once, twice, three times. But it was the cool press of the fangs against my opening that jerked my hips up into his seeking mouth, my orgasm ripping from my mouth in a scream that Nathan caught in a kiss.

Cole gently pressed his forearm against my lower stomach and shot his tongue into my core, spearing it as he lightly bit along my labia...and another orgasm shattered me as he speared his tongue in and out of me over and over, finishing me by lapping at my entrance, slick with my orgasms and his attentions.

Nathan released my mouth reluctantly and Cole sat up and away from me. I lay there with my legs spread before a stranger, a vampire. Who had just given me the best sex of my life without using his cock. He bent over me once more and kissed my most private part and I shivered, my hips moving of their own accord. He worked his way up my body, my hand rising to press against his head and his hips lay cradled between my open legs and I could feel his arousal between them.

"Why didn't you take me?" I asked. Mad, frightened and sexually frustrated all in one confused mess.

"You are not yourself right now. I would not have our first time like this, when blood-languor is upon you. It will be your choice who you mate with, and Alexander's." A cloud of some dark emotion crossed his face at the mention of the leader's name.

With a tender finger along my jaw he said, "You taste perfect, *you are perfect*." He kissed me. I could taste myself on his mouth and it made me moan underneath him and he shuddered.

"You undo me. I must go." Nathan was above me and looked longingly at what Cole had just done.

Cole straightened my panties and skirt. "You must be hungry."

Not anymore, I thought dreamily. My core throbbed for something other than food.

Nathan shook his head. "Let us take her to the Gathering Room."

I was very woozy after the blood loss and the sex. Each man helped me to my feet, one on either side. My eyes found the shattered cell phone and I pulled out of Cole's grip, my senses beginning to right themselves.

"I texted my friend." I snatched my hand out of his, backing away from both of them, the aftereffects of the bloodletting slipping away in a rush. "You know...the one you let the cop rape."

Cole's expression darkened and my gaze went to his mouth, thinking about where it had been but minutes before. A flush rose to my face. I was trapped with these two men. I had allowed one of them to do things to me and I was instantly angry. How could I have let him? Them?

I stomped to the door, catching myself from falling against the jamb. Cole was instantly there, supporting my elbow. "You are not at your full strength. You need to eat. We could do nothing for your friend."

"Yeah, I know...cattle," I said, tearing my arm away from him and glaring at Nathan. They stared back at me, Nathan reaching forward and opening the door.

I walked in the hallway and immediately felt unsure of myself but my residual anger from being bled, manipulated and essentially used sexually while I was physically vulnerable fueled me onward. I swung around, still dizzy and leaned against the wall, my vision dimming, my anger and frustration at my circumstance burning hot tears in my eyes that refused to fall.

Cole got real close to me and whispered in my ear, "You are not well, let me carry you."

I shook my head and my vision swam in streamers of color. He was definitely not going to touch me again. I ground my teeth together as I began to slide down the wall, my palm dragging against the cold stone.

"Just pick her up!" Nathan said.

Cole did, easily scooping me up in his arms and I hit him in his chest with weak fists. "Put me down..." my head lolled against him and the first, hot tears stained his black shirt and I fainted where I lay, safely pressed against him.

8

I stirred, waking in another room with Eve peering anxiously over me.

"They should have never bled you before you had taken food," she said, patting my forehead with a damp cloth.

Hunger slammed into me when I smelled a bowl of something that made my taste buds come alive in a roaring inferno.

I sat up too quickly and dizziness assaulted me. Nausea kicked in and I said, "I think I'm going to be sick." I slammed my feet down on the cold floor and ran to the bathroom, but my weakness caused me to stumble and I put my hands out to brace my fall and I was in his arm's again.

Cole's.

I was too weak to struggle and lay there, my stomach heaving from blood loss and lack of food.

"You fool! She can hardly walk…she is sick to her stomach! Could you have not waited?" Eve yelled at him and I lay still, listening for a heartbeat that wasn't there.

I watched Cole's eyes close, the iciness gone for a moment then he looked down at me. "Forgive me, I would not harm you purposely."

I was too tired to be angry. I said nothing and he sighed but the urge to throw up had passed.

"Give me the soup. I will feed her."

Eve pursed her lips and gave him the bowl. Cole carried me to where I had lain, using only one arm, the soup in the other hand.

He sat down and tenderly brought me to a sitting position and my stomach lurched. Instinctively I put a hand over my mouth.

He scooped up some of the fragrant broth and lifted it to my mouth and I parted my lips for him and a fine sweat appeared above his lip. It was then that I knew that he wanted me for himself. It didn't matter what their leader (Alexander) thought, this vampire would be as territorial as he needed to be.

I would use that as leverage and escape this place. It didn't matter that the sex was great. The fringe benefits weren't sounding too hot at the moment. I ate half a bowl and allowed my head to fall back against his chest again, playing the weak female card for all it was worth.

It wasn't that hard.

He clenched me tighter and stroked my hair.

Eve said, "Don't get attached to her. You know better. Alexander will make a match that is best for a breeding pair..."

"I know that better than most!" he spoke to her harshly and she cringed away from him.

"Have you stopped to think that the Druids should not be matched for biology solely, but for love?"

Eve shook her head. "You know that is not the way of it, Cole. Think with your head," I watched her press a fingertip to her temple, "not your emotions. You have always been thus."

"I am not ashamed that I wished to be mated to a Druid and not share her with others."

"That will never happen," Eve said. "At the very least, she will have two mates. It cannot be avoided, there are too few."

Cole let out a frustrated breath and it moved my hair, his arms crushed me to him and I smiled.

Gotcha.

I had regained some strength and Eve managed to convince them all that I was ready to partake in the ceremony. Albeit after there was something solid in my stomach.

I approached the cavernous room, noise echoing and bouncing off the walls. There were many women (and some men) lined up at a huge banquet table piling food on plates.

Many of the women were pregnant.

Many looked alike.

Druids, I thought. It was the first time I had ever felt a sense of belonging. Momentarily, I felt a comfort but the life I'd had came crashing down on me. This was some kidnap worship crap and I needed to stick to the plan. I needed to pretend, and get out of here. My eyes flitted around from one person to the next, finally landing on the huge vampire leader, Alexander.

He wasted no time, moving toward me in a rush, his actions a blur. I had a sense of vertigo as he approached and steadied myself against the wall I had stuck close to.

Another vampire, who looked vaguely familiar held a plate of food. Vegetables, roasted chicken and a small amount of fruit sat atop it and he handed it to me without a word, his eyes watching the pulse which beat in my throat as if mesmerized.

"Cole has told me what has happened."

I blushed a fine, true red. Completely embarrassed about him knowing the intimate details of the sexual encounter that transpired between Cole and I and to a lesser degree, Nathan.

I put my chin down and refused to meet his eyes, he lifted it with a finger. "Let me introduce you, Pureblood."

He didn't know, I thought. I looked around for Cole and there he was in the shadows of the room, watching me covertly. His gaze was a weight on my body. I shivered at the look he sent me and tried to calm myself.

My body remembered how it felt to have that sultry attention, betraying me even as I angered. I looked away hurriedly, following Alexander out into the center of the room, my hand gripped in his.

"This is Rachel Collins. She is the first pureblood Druid to enter our kiss in one hundred years." There were murmurings all around. Apparently, it was big news. I stood there waiting.

Finally, Alexander gestured for me to sit and I did gratefully, taking small bites of my meal and realizing I was starving. I ate as quickly as I could.

The food stuck in my throat as five vampires came to stand before Alexander.

"Two of these vampires will be your mates. Maybe... more."

I shook my head, my stomach lurching in a sickening way. "I didn't say I wanted them."

Alexander frowned, I guess he wasn't used to a "no." But I had to play along so I rushed on, explaining, "I want to have a choice." I looked and saw Cole glower. He thought I'd be choosing someone else.

I was choosing to escape but that was for later, for now I would play along.

"Let us see who amongst these are a good breeding selection for you."

I stood and walked to the vampires, my heart racing. They were all huge males, *vampires*. The eyes were the same, they watched me with anticipation and I approached them warily. What would this mean?

Nathan was among them and suddenly I felt cold. I repressed an almost insane urge to look for Cole. Why was he not amongst them?

They circled me. One came from behind and another came forward pinning my arms to my side and crushing his lips to mine. "Submit, Druid," he said, his hand going right for my crotch. I squirmed against steel bands and struggled, hardly able to breathe. They weren't doing anything, they were no better than the men that Cole had saved me from.

"She has such spirit, look at how she tries to fight." He tore at my panties and began to dig his way inside me and I threw my head forward into his and he stumbled back, his hand retreating while I was bodily picked up by the vampire behind me, swung around and pressed to the floor. My head was ringing and the vampire I'd hit was coming toward me again to join in some kind of gang-rape.

I screamed and Cole was there, his fangs bared and his arm shooting out. His hand wrapped the throat of the vampire that rode me, his knees spreading my legs.

Cole lifted him by his throat, heaving him into the stone wall and I scrambled backward on all fours until I was pressed against Cole's shins.

"Alexander, how can you allow this?" Cole yelled as Nathan held back the other three that would have rushed Cole.

"Calm down, Reaper. You know she must be used by all so that she may become pregnant right away. Can you not smell her, she is fertile."

Cole said nothing and Alexander's eyes narrowed. "You do know. Have you been with her?"

Cole shook his head. I whimpered and pressed my face harder against him and he moved his legs apart so I fit more securely against them.

"Let them have her, Cole. She may choose a mate. Afterward."

The one that Cole had thrown watched me at Cole's feet like a feral animal.

"Please, don't let them have me," I pleaded up at him, and his eyes held mine and I had a stab of guilt, knowing my intent was to leave this place and use whatever emotional attachment he had for me against him.

"I will check her fertility," Alexander said and Cole growled, his fangs tearing out of their encasement of flesh.

"You will step away from the Druid, Reaper."

Cole relented with a grunt of disgust and I was left alone on the middle of the floor as Alexander approached me.

He wasted no time getting down on the floor, between my legs as a hundred people looked on he lifted my skirt and plunged a finger inside me, moving it back and forth. I tried to close my legs but he easily pressed them apart. His breathing came faster as he positioned himself between my legs using his other hand to pull down his pants.

Cole, from so much closer than I thought, said quietly, "You are not to have her either, Alexander."

Alexander slid his hand out of the slickness of me and I swept my legs closed, knowing every vampire in the room had seen what Alexander had. The vampires had their eyes latched to me, pupils dilated.

Alexander stood, fastening his pants with shaking hands. "I forgot myself."

All eyes turned to me and I kept my legs together and tried to look as appealing and vulnerable as I could, it was all the leverage that I had. Nathan was especially enthralled, licking his lips and waiting for his chance.

The other Druids looked on with horror as Cole came and lifted me to a standing position on shaky feet. I couldn't stop the naked accusation that filled my eyes. We had managed to stave off the inevitable only because Alexander himself lost control. As the leader, he was looking pretty bad right about now.

I could still feel his probing fingers inside me and couldn't contain an involuntary shudder.

All that talk about what a precious commodity Druid Breeders were was lost before his lust. The female vampires looked at me like something to squash underneath their heel.

Wonderful position I was in. Leaving sooner rather than later would be better.

"She has three days of fertility. You know the rites, Cole. She will have to submit to five Reapers. It is the way. After, she can be mated with two," Alexander shrugged, his momentary faux pas, like a pink elephant in the room, forgotten.

Cole wasn't going to forget. I could sense it, tasting his reluctance to comply like a fine wine on my tongue.

9

The community supper had been awkward as hell and I had suffered through it while taking furtive glances at the five that were going to gang rape me in front of everyone.

I wanted them in my sights.

I ground through my meal, knowing I must eat in anticipation of fleeing this place. I wasn't going to stay any longer than I must. When I was eating I sat between Cole and Eve, who kept a diligent eye on what I consumed. I covertly scanned the room and picked up on the other Druids. They seemed easy and sure, their vampire males doting on them. Some women seemed to have two or three partners. I couldn't believe they could accept this life. A life where a different specifies held them captive and bred them like prized mules.

It wasn't for me.

Eve and Cole walked me back to my room and I could feel the other vampires' eyes on my back the entire length of the hall.

I turned when we reached the door. "Why in front of everyone?"

Cole understood exactly what I was asking.

"We have had some issues in the past. It is best that a coupling happen in full view initially so there cannot be question as to whom has had a rightful turn," he shrugged with clear distaste cloaking his face.

I had to ask and I could see in Eve's eyes her burning desire for me not to.

"Why were you not amongst them? Why didn't you warn me?" I thought of Alexander's unwanted fingers inside me and my face leaked my thoughts all over the place.

He looked pained (if a vampire can look that way). "I asked him to hold off. I explained about some of our… activities and the taking of the blood. Alexander indicated he would wait."

"But he didn't tell you outright."

He shook his head. "He thinks I've become too attached to you. He thinks I am too 'alpha' to be in a breeding pair."

"Alpha?" I asked, my eyebrow cocked and I heard Eve sigh.

"Some of the vampires don't have the disposition to share their mates," she expounded.

Cole glowered.

Eve looked up at him. "You brought it on yourself, Reaper. She is ready, fertile. You stumbled upon her in a dangerous situation from which you extracted her. Don't forget your duty to your race. Do not be as the *rogue*."

Cole glared at her but she continued, turning to me, "Alpha is the way they all are, it is a natural disposition for vampires. But some are born with an extra portion." She was talking to me but looking at him.

"Fine." He looked at the two of us. "I could not stand by and watch her being mauled. She needs more time. That is one thing that the *rogue* believe: that she should have a choice."

"You saw Alexander, he will not give her too much more. She has what? Two days? Leave Cole. Do a mission, find another of Druid blood. Ease the sting from our leaders' decisions by bringing more to this place. Be gone for the rite."

"Wait…you are what…getting women all the time?" I asked. Wondering about this faction of vampires that did not live with them. That were outcast, that disobeyed rules.

He nodded. "It is what Nathan and I do. We scout."

"Reapers…" I whispered, my comprehension complete.

He saw my expression and nodded acquiescence. "We harvest."

And with that, he walked away, his leathers marking his progress in the hollow emptiness of the hall.

10

I lay awake in my small bed while the moonlight illumi-
nated the bones of the furniture that stood at stark attention in the shadowed corners. Eve had elaborated about the
rogue. They did not believe that Druids should be shared,
they wished to not follow the "old ways." But, Eve warned,
they also took Druids, and mated with them…and forced
them to stay with them. They killed whatever vampires
that stood in their way. Vampire scouts like Cole and
Nathan would be killed on sight and a small battle would
ensue to ascertain their success. The scouts were at their
most vulnerable after they'd acquired a Druid. The chance
of a *rogue* on their tail was high.

I deliberated. That was why I had hardly been at the
police station for any length of time. If they'd scented me
out, the *rogue* would not have been far behind. Effectively
shadowing the trail left by the Reapers.

A soft knock sounded at my door and a female vamp
walked in. Taller than I at almost six foot she approached

the bed and I warily scooted back against the wall, the pillow between cushioning me from the coldness of the stone.

She held up a palm in placation. "Fear not, Druid. I wish to help you and thereby help myself." She attempted a smile but when her fangs were revealed I cringed at the sight and the smile faded.

Her lips were terribly red and my eyes latched onto them as my heart beat harder.

She exhaled a shaky breath and I realized that she was fighting her thirst.

She began without preamble, "I desire to be with Cole. I have mixed ancestry and may be able to breed." She seemed to need an answer so I nodded slowly. The crazy bitch. Who was I to argue?

She took my silence as acceptance and went on, "I have brought some things for you to wear to help you escape this place. You will be unable to return to your rightful home. They will try to reacquire you there…"

She trailed off and looked at me.

Hope glowed in my eyes that was impossible to dim. I *so* wanted out of here and here she was handing it to me on a silver platter.

An image of Cole entered my mind and I shoved it aside. *Stick to the plan, Rachel*, I chanted to myself.

She leaned forward and from behind her back she slowly pushed clothing and a small pack onto my lap. I was so thrilled with the prospect I missed her hand as it snaked out, coiling around my throat. My neck felt like a flower stem that had been caught in the mouth of a lion.

I didn't move as her mouth lingered over mine and issued the warning, "Do not return, Druid."

I moved my chin up and down and she released me. Her long fingers trailed softly along my collarbone as she moved away.

It stole my breath.

She backed away from me with her hand planted over her nose. When she reached the doorway she paused with her other hand on the frame.

"Change and go to the furthest door at the end of the hall. It will be unlocked. After you pass through, follow the wall at your left and there will be a gate at its end." She looked into my eyes and I could feel her pressing her will on me.

It was ineffective because I was a pureblood. I did a mental eye-roll.

She huffed her frustration. "It will be unlatched as well."

"Wait," I called after her bravely.

She turned and her pale eyes glittered against the moonlight reflectively and I flinched, thinking again of a lion. "Why do you want him?"

She smiled and it was menacing, not happy. "He is a fine warrior and will breed true, every female wishes to mate with him. He is not like the others." Her expression changed. She was reconsidering my rescue and maybe substituting it with my death. I saw her mind mulling it over.

I interrupted her thought process, "I'll go."

"Self-preservation. Very good." She turned on her heel and silently left the room.

I slunk down the dark hall dimly lit with sconces that flick-ered with candlelight. I knew that every vampire in the compound must be awake but not one was anywhere to be seen.

I let out a shaky breath and continued, the moonlight streaming through the windows lighting the path before me. My hand glided down the wall and the rough texture of the stone tore softly at the flesh of my palm as I neared the door.

Once there I could not see a handle or latch and felt around until I found a cup-like indentation carved along the side where it met the frame. Scooping my finger inside it I pulled.

It didn't move.

I pushed and it slid open soundlessly. The night air rushed in and robbed me of breath. It was so cold that I stood stock still. Huddling inside the parka that the female vampire had given me, I made my way along the outside wall, using my left hand to space myself and the moonlight to secure my steps.

As I came to the end of the wall I saw the gate, slightly ajar and standing in a sea of stone that was a wall ten feet high.

I moved to the door and gave it brief examination as I slid through. It would not have been something I could have moved. It reminded me of stories I had heard about castles with moats and such, it was formidable, tall, rough-hewn and too heavy to swing.

She had left it open, my mind supplied unhelpfully. Better not to dwell on the strength disparity between me and her.

In fact, maybe I should hustle my ass along before she changed her mind.

I did, making my way into a wooded glade with only the moonlight to guide me.

11

I felt like I'd been walking for miles (I probably had). My feet screamed and I decided that I'd made enough distance that I could safely rest and inspect my pack.

There wasn't a lot I noticed, rummaging around. I had a bottle of water and a sandwich. I was sure it was whatever had been left over from the elaborate banquet. A feeling of unease stole over me as I thought about the female more. She had packed hardly anything. Yet, she hadn't killed me. It was puzzling and my mind felt as if it was circling the answer but hadn't reached the center of the maze yet.

I ate half the sandwich and was recapping the water when I stood and stretched, throwing the pack on my back and readying myself to locate a road. Distantly, I could hear traffic. I'd walked for, I looked at my watch and figured two hours; maybe five miles or so?

A small noise startled me and my heart sank when I saw five vampires exit the woods in a loose circle around me.

None of them looked familiar. But I knew they were Vampire, my body tingled in recognition. Their clothes, bearing, everything was different from the compound I'd just been in.

Their eyes shone like onyx in the moonlight.

That's when it hit me, their irises were not silvered like the others, but shone like blood does in the dark.

Black.

The *rogue*.

I ran.

The backpack bounced on my back as I fled, the branches crashing and whipping at my body as I pushed through the dense tree cover, the cold biting my hands, nipping them painfully.

I was roughly pulled from behind by my hair and I yelped before a hand covered my mouth.

Pulling me in against his body a vampire said, "Quiet, breeder. We have lost your trail only to be reunited."

"Zach, can you believe our luck?" another one said off to my right.

"Actually, I cannot," he said, running his fangs up and down my neck as he kept it taut and long, using my hair to turn me as he wished.

I realized the female vampire hadn't been so crazy after all. She sent me out here as bait. She knew the *rogue* would be after me like sharks in the water, scenting blood. She could wash her hands of my death, feign innocence when asked and know I'd been dispatched. I was out of her hair and she could have Cole.

I despaired.

The one they called Zach released me abruptly and I stumbled, pinwheeling my arms as I almost fell. I rubbed my head where it was sore from his treatment and tried to keep the remaining four in sight.

For all the goddamn good it would do. They were fast and unbelievably strong. If they wanted to play cat and mouse, I was sorta out of options.

"We almost had you…" Zach said, coming toward me slowly, his saunter showing me he was in charge and there was no escape.

No options. I squelched my feelings of hopelessness. I had never given up on anything in my life. I wasn't going to give in without a fight.

Where was the sun when I needed it? That'd fry their asses. I looked at the moon, riding full and high above me and scowled as I massaged my scalp.

He laughed and the other vamps did with him, the eeriness of it echoing in the openness of the meadow that was surrounded by trees. "It will not be daylight for how long…" he tapped his finger on his head with the beat of my heart.

He whirled on me and my heart skipped a beat while he laughed again. "I do hear it, Breeder."

My heartbeat. He was listening to it.

I backed up until I could feel the tree biting against my back, the sharp bark a comfort against me.

"Two hours more until dawn. We will squire you away safely by then," another said.

Zach's face grew serious as he said, "Have they had you yet, Breeder?"

I could feel the blush rise to my cheeks, the heat of it a burning torture. Was there nothing I could have that was private? I thought of Cole, he would have been a safer bet than this group.

I sighed. "No."

One of them cackled in delight and another male said, "Alexander must have had to put it in a knothole to keep it out of this one!"

Charming. The whole group. "You jerks must be the *rogue*," I said with a bravado I didn't feel. The one that had just made the crack narrowed his black eyes to slits and in a rush was up against my body, his hand latched to my breast. I cried out, I couldn't help it.

"Not so brave now, Breeder, with my hand feeding on your tit," and for emphasis he squeezed it just on the good side of pain and I whimpered. He smiled as his other hand went for my crotch.

"Leave her," Zach said dismissively. "There is plenty of time to partake of the breeder upon our return. Besides, where she is, they will follow."

Reluctantly he took his hands off my body and placed them above my head on the tree bark. He went in to sniff my neck and I leaned away from him.

"This one smells of something different," he said. Serious now, where before he'd been playing games with my raw nerves.

Zach was near me in record time, his dark colored clothes a gray blur as he moved. I closed my eyes and moved my head to the side, both vamps at either side of my neck, skimming the flesh with their faces.

Finally Zach raised his head and the other vampire said, "What is it?"

Zach shook his head. "It cannot be. But it is," he leaned forward and ran the length of his fangs along my neck, piercing it with the barest of strokes.

A single drop of blood flowed down my neck and his tongue flicked out and captured it as my tears fell down my face. They trembled at my jaw and fell on his cheek as he came away with his blood prize.

Zach's eyes flicked to my face as I stood staring up at him. He straightened, a small fleck of ruby on his lip, looking like a black dot in the night.

"Pureblood," he said.

The others crowded around me but he held up a hand. "We need to exit this place immediately." He looked around at each face gravely. "They will never stop hunting for this one." He grasped my chin in his hand and moved my face from side to side. "Matthew," he called softly, never looking away.

"Yes?"

"Let her ride on your back, we will run."

I broke free again, taking them by surprise but they were on me in a flash and I struggled underneath the one that had pawed my body.

Finally I screamed, "Get off me!" in his face and he backhanded me playfully. It made my ears ring and I saw stars.

And it had been a light touch.

"You heard her, viper, get off."

Cole.

I hiccuped back a sob of gratitude so loud that it echoed in the meadow, the silence swallowing it whole.

They backed away from me, all except the one that had been on me. He fisted his hand in my hair and dragged me after him. I screamed. It felt like pinpoints of fire bursting all over my scalp.

I was vaguely aware of something flying over my head, coming over my body in a wash of muted color and then my hair was released, leaving my scalp to throb to the beat of my heart.

I heard a protracted gurgling behind me and cautiously opened my eyes and saw Cole, his thumbs buried to the connective tissue through my attacker's throat. The remaining group surrounded him.

"Cole…" I rasped, "look out!"

He stood, all lean and heavily muscled grace as Zach, Matthew and the two which remained closed in around him. I scuttled back against a tree to watch.

Zach came at Cole and the two collided, each grappling for the other. Matthew put a choke hold on Cole and the two others began sharp jabs at his torso.

Cole head butted Matthew from behind and he stumbled away, blood spraying from his nose. Cole punched Zach in the jaw with his free arm and he staggered while Cole tore the arm off the one holding his arm with a wet pop. An arterial spray of blood shot up in the night sky like black oil. I began to feel shocky as I watched it all unfold. Like I was having an out-of-body experience. I could hear this strange wheezing sound and I belatedly realized it was me.

Zach began to savagely jab Cole in the side while the other vampire came for me. Waking out of my stupor I leaped up and flung myself behind the tree but he was faster. He lashed around with his wrist and grabbed my arm, pulling me with such force I gasped at the pain, so much more than anything I'd ever experienced and he jerked me to him. I came easily into his embrace, all loose limbs and in a haze of pain that stole my strength to scream.

Cole heard me. He laced his hands together and drove them into Zach's face and he slumped forward. Cole caught him, pushing him away from his body like so much trash.

Those silvered eyes fell on the vampire that held me. They flashed with fire and rage and I felt his arms stiffen about me as he debated on the merits of my life versus his.

His won.

He let me slide down his body and with a moan I lay at his feet, my shoulder a throbbing nightmare. At this point I didn't care if they killed me. I hurt so bad and my arm was numb from wrist to shoulder.

I watched Cole come for him. He tried to fight him off but Cole was the superior fighter and finally the ratio was fair. Cole dispatched him by slamming his head on the tree so hard his skull split and his brains splattered on the trunk where my body had been.

As if in a dream, his face appeared above me. His buzzed head and curled tattoos winding alongside his neck looked like black claws. His eyes held mine as he tenderly ran a finger down my jaw.

"Why did you run, Rachel?" his voice asked, sounding like grinding rocks.

I shook my head. It didn't seem like he'd kill me but... "A female..." I sucked in a breath and continued, "she told me to leave, she wanted you. And I wanted to get out of there. I don't want..."

"Shh..." he said and looked at my shoulder, frowning.

"He has torn some ligaments and muscle," he observed as he probed my shoulder and I shrieked in agony.

"I am sorry." He looked behind him at where Zachary lay then turned to me. "He is not dead and we must go. It will feel terrible to move you but we need to make haste before sunrise."

I nodded. Anything to make the pain end, I thought in a daze.

He gently pushed his arms underneath my body and lifted me like I weighed nothing. Of course, the vampires could bench press small cars, my weight probably didn't register.

Nathan came into the clearing and they regarded one another.

"How does she fare?"

"She is damaged, they have hurt her shoulder…"

"Did they…?" Nathan cocked an eyebrow.

"No. Insufficient time. They will not again." Cole shook his head. He had made sure.

"You can't come back, you know," Nathan said.

Cole nodded. "I know. But they will not have her. I cannot abide…" he sighed in frustration.

Nathan held up a hand. "I understand, my brother. Fear not, I will say only what I see here." He looked at him steadily. "I will miss you."

"And I, you."

They looked at each other, then at the sky, which was a soft black. It heralded the day to come.

"Where will you go?"

Cole shrugged. "Somewhere unknown."

"He may hunt you. And then, there is the *rogue*…"

"Let me concern myself with Alexander and his. The *rogue* is another matter entirely."

"You know how to meet me should you wish contact," Nathan said.

"I do. Thank you, Nathan."

"You are most welcome." Nathan walked over to me and I stared at him with wide, pain-filled eyes. "She is a gem," his eyes flicked to Cole's. "Take care of her. She may be our future."

Cole replied, "She is. My future."

I listened to them through my pain and knew that my life was forever changing. I thought of Michelle, my job, my life as I'd known it—gone. I was captured by this man, this vampire. Born of blood and thirst and myself with an uncertain genetic code that mastered my destiny into what it had become.

Nathan looked at me one last time and then turning, he melted into the dark forest.

12

ole ran with me in his arms. It was graceful considering the awkwardness of the hold and him taking every back trail in existence. Finally we were skirting around the city and he set me on my feet where the woods ended and suburbia merged with the perimeter.

I swayed where I stood, my shoulder a throbbing wasteland of pain. I bit my lip to keep from crying but useless tears fell as I stood there.

Cole brought me into his body. "We need to make haste to your dwelling and assemble your belongings to take with us." He looked at the neat lawn of a human's backyard and returned his gaze to mine. "I think there may be something I can do to ease your suffering, heal what was done to you. I am sorry I could not stop it."

I shook my head, negating his guilt. "You killed them so they couldn't take me." I swiped a tear away using my good arm. "If it hadn't been for you, I'd be with them even now. I'd be going from the frying pan to the fire."

I twisted in his arms to look into his face and he cocked an eyebrow.

I smiled. "I'd go from one bad situation to another."

"Ah." He nodded in understanding.

He gathered me to him again like a precious commodity.

We made our way to my apartment, which was located on the top floor. When we arrived at the door I saw the bright yellow crime scene tape barring it like a sad ribbon.

I frowned, remembering my text with Michelle. So, the cops *had* crawled all over my apartment. I let out a breath and looked at Cole.

But he only had eyes for our surroundings. He was scanning every dark corner of the hall. Expecting the devil to spring out like a jack-in-the-box.

He tried the knob and it was locked. He gave a vicious twist and it snapped apart and the door swung soundlessly inward.

Moonlight filled the inside of the apartment and I swung my good arm to hit the light switch but Cole grabbed my wrist softly. "Do not."

Right, don't alert the troops I'm back. Duh. I let my arm drop to my side and went straight to my medicine cabinet. I caught my reflection in the mirror. Startled pale blue eyes floated above what looked like bruises from the combination of lack of sleep and pain. I opened the cabinet quickly and grabbed the Ibuprofen. Grabbing three, I slugged them back with some water, gulping greedily. My nose felt cold and my hands shook with the effort to not go into shock, get warm, stay sane.

I shut the cabinet and Cole was in the reflection behind me. I yelped and dropped the bottle.

"I did not mean to startle you," Cole said, putting a hand on my shoulder and I winced.

His eyes met mine in the mirror and he moved his hand up my neck while bending down until his lips met where his hand had been. I sighed, loving the feel of his palm on my flesh.

I turned into him and he kissed the fragile length of me, his lips moving to my jaw and working their way until they were pressed against my mouth. He worked over the top of them, lifting and feeding off them until they felt almost swollen.

He pulled me into his arms and lifted me. He took me to my bed and laid me down. His large hands brushed the few hairs that impeded his kisses away.

But he did not kiss me, instead he said, "I will heal you now."

He removed my parka, which was a terrible struggle made even more so with the slowness necessary to keep the arm immobile. I bit my lip and whimpered. I hated my weakness but couldn't help it. He lowered his head to kiss me, raining soft pressure on my face, cheekbones, everywhere his mouth touched he worshiped me with it.

Finally, when Cole thought that he'd given me enough of a reprieve, he removed the most difficult part and I screamed my pain and he captured it with his mouth, gently pushing me back onto the bed.

His warm mouth left mine and he got a pair of scissors and cut off the shirt so my bare skin was revealed. As was the delicate lace of my crimson bra. His eyes held mine then traveled across my breasts and finally to the wounded shoulder.

He placed his palm on my shoulder and I gasped. His flesh felt feverishly hot. I started to pull away and he looked at me. "Keep still, Rachel."

I stayed where I was by sheer willpower. The heat radiated from the point of contact and spread throughout my entire body. At once the shoulder ceased its endless throbbing, which was replaced with heat. The warmth radiated and as the pressure increased from his hands there was an interior explosion of pain and my body bucked, fighting the sensation.

I looked up at him with frightened eyes. He reassured me, "Your body is mending the wound."

"Why does it hurt?" I asked in a small voice.

Cole shrugged and the leather he wore rubbed against itself, making a pleasant crackling sound I'd always associate with him.

It went on forever but when I glanced at the clock it had only taken twenty minutes. It was nearly five in the morning.

Daylight was coming.

Cole saw me look at the clock. "Almost...there," he said, his hands easing on my shoulder. They began to make lazy, light circles in the injured area and I clenched my fingers as he lifted his hands from me.

I sat up and rotated my shoulder, lifting it to my ear in an exaggerated shrug then letting it fall.

A stupid grin filled my face.

I watched Cole grin at me for the first time, his fangs glowing softly in the faded moonlight that speared my room.

A feeling of happiness burst within me for this man.

The vampire.

Some of the worst of my tiredness began to fall away as the pain left. I got to my knees and hugged him around his neck. His arms wrapped around me instantly and I breathed into his ear, "I want to be with you."

He pulled away and it was the only time I'd seen his face soft. "And I you. Had you stayed, I could have helped you. Do not run again."

I laughed. "I don't think you have to worry about that."

We gazed into each other's eyes, making an unspoken commitment.

My breath caught in my throat as Cole stiffened in my arms, his eyes widening.

I looked over my shoulder and there stood Erik with a gun.

The creeper from my work.

Cole pushed me violently away from him and turned to Erik and that's when I saw it. A dart stuck out of his back like an evil exclamation point.

Zach filled my doorway and saw me lying on the bed.

Cole staggered into Erik, trying to get the gun and Erik shot him again.

I jumped off the bed and Zach calmly walked around the bed and pointed a gun to my chest.

I threw my hands up and screamed, "No!"

Too late, Cole, drugged and slowed, threw his fist into Zach's temple. But the force was too little. Zach turned and used both hands to shove Cole halfway across the room. He landed against the wall, dazed. A huge dent caved in where he'd hit.

Erik said, "I want to fuck her bad." His eyes swung to the bed as I rushed to where Cole lay. His head lolled to the side and his eyes were glazing over.

Zach gave Erik a look and he cringed away from him. He stalked over to us and crouched down to face Cole, their faces inches away from each other. He grabbed a fistful of Cole's black shirt and jerked his face even closer. "You should have killed me when you had the chance, Reaper. Know this…she will be mine within the week."

Cole struggled weakly and tried to grab me to him but Zach chuckled, wresting me away from his weak grasp.

"I gave him enough tranquilizer to put two elephants to sleep. He'll be out when the sun rises; a crispy critter in three hours," Erik said with smug satisfaction.

I was wrapped in Zach's arms and didn't struggle, my heart felt like a dead lump in my chest.

The first, hot tear made its way down my face. It trembled on my jaw then fell onto the hands that held me captive. My eyes never left Cole's. He shook his head like a dazed bull, trying to rid himself of the fog that he found himself in.

Struggling to stand, Erik came to Cole and slammed the butt of the tranquilizer gun into his temple.

I screamed as Cole staggered back against the wall.

"Enough," Zach said. "You have your uses, Intimate. Don't make me rethink them."

Erik was breathing heavily, I could see he wanted to lay into Cole but Zach was his master here.

Erik looked at me. "You're so stupid. The *rogue* used me for months to spy on you. They were just waiting for the perfect opportunity to take you from underneath their noses," he said, gesturing with the gun at Cole.

"You talk too much. Your singular job is to watch the Reaper. If he moves, shoot him."

"He ain't gonna move. He has two darts stuck in him!"

Zach's hand lashed out so fast I couldn't track it but Erik's head rocked back and he stumbled. A spot of blood appeared at the corner of his mouth.

"Do not underestimate the Reapers. They are the elite of the Vampire. He will try to reacquire this one. It appears that he has bonded with her. Fool...do you not understand what that means?"

Clearly, Erik did not but continued to give Zach his sullen regard.

"As long as he lives, he will seek her."

"Then let me do him right now!" Erik said in frustration.

Zach shook his head. "It is best to leave him. Let him live or not. Let the others deal with him. He is as sought as us now. He cannot return after he has bonded with this female. He is obliged to share in his kiss. Correct?" Zach swung his gaze to Cole.

Cole just stared back at him.

Zach dragged me backwards and Erik trained the gun on Cole. Cole's dull eyes were full of rage and grief as they flicked from the human that held the gun on him to mine, anguished.

Zach laughed at Cole's look and he surged forward.

To rescue me.

I watched in slow motion as Erik depressed the trigger, the meaty sound of the impact striking through the inky cloth of Cole's shirt.

The light died in his eyes, as he slid down the wall.

Erik looked at me with triumph and turned to Zach.

I struggled to get away, to go to Cole, to be away from Erik and the *rogue*.

It was futile. I was tossed over his shoulder as they moved down the stairs. As we exited the stairwell I saw the long black SUV waiting at the curb.

Smoke from its exhaust curled lazily in the chilled night air. Erik opened the door and from my view it looked like a huge mouth waiting to swallow me whole.

I beat at Zach with my fists and he held me to him so tightly I couldn't breathe. Finally when he tired of my struggling he looked at Erik. "Give it to me."

An evil smile overcame his face from the front seat and he handed back a cloth soaked with something foul. Zach covered my face with it and my last thought was of Cole. I was in the hands of the enemy.

The *rogue.*

I saw, as if through dark water, a huge figure stagger down the staircase, a blurred silhouette in black.

Zach saw him too and a smile curled his mouth. With two fingers he pointed them ahead of the car and said to the driver, "Go...now."

Cole rushed the car as it sped away and the last words I heard before consciousness left me was, "You did not use near enough tranquilizer."

Cole's howls followed me down into the endless spiral of unconsciousness and I knew no more.

BLED
Volume Two: The Druid Series
Copyright © 2011 Marata Eros

THE
DRUID 2
SERIES
BLED

MARATA EROS

1

I awoke with the feeling of an iron spike being driven through my right eyeball, my throat a parched desert. I cracked open an eyelid. Being careful not to move my head too quickly I took stock of my surroundings.

It was déjà vu for sure. I was back in another room, but there was no stone on these walls. It was homey and comfortable. There was just one problem.

Erik.

The putz from work was leaning up against the wall, one heel propped up behind him. He pushed off when he saw that I was awake and sauntered over to the bed. A satisfied smile proclaimed his smugness.

"Hey sleepy-head. Finally, you're awake," he said, reaching out as if to touch me.

"Don't touch me dickhead," I said through my teeth.

"Brave words, considering your position here." He indicated my hands that were bound behind my back.

I tugged and felt the material bite into my wrists, my feet were unbound.

"I bet ya your vamp boss won't like you working me over when he's not around," I said, raising my chin defiantly.

His smirk fell away. "He's left it up to me, I'm in charge of you while my master's away." I watched his hands flex and clench.

Creepy Erik didn't like that.

Good to know.

"Why don't you be a good little slave and fetch me some food?" Maybe he'd do something to me I could survive but would get him off watchdog duty. It would be great if he wasn't around. I didn't trust him, he made my skin creep off my body.

He whipped his slicked back hair off his face and leaned down close to me, his rancid breath preceding his words, "Watch it, I can do what I want with you while the Master isn't here." He reached out and grabbed my breast.

He gave my tit a painful crank until he got the reaction out of me that he wanted. I whimpered and he released me, my breast felt like it was on fire and a heat rose to my face. I wasn't embarrassed, no way. Any man that would grope a woman, a bound woman, was a coward.

I was steaming pissed.

"If ya don't want more of that, you'll keep your smart yap shut."

I waited until he was leaning away, a little off-balance and swung my leg into his ugly retreating face, smashing the side of my foot into the bridge of his nose and blood sprayed out in an arc, splattering me.

"You bitch!" he hollered. One palm smashed against his nose to stymie the flow, his other balled into a fist. He moved toward me and I turned my head at the last critical moment as his fist rose above me like a dark moon. I squeezed my eyes, anticipating the blow.

Some small sound alerted me and my eyes flew open.

Zach stood there, the fist that had been raised to abuse, held in a hand that was twice as big, his onyx eyes boring into mine.

"Argh...! Let me go!" Erik screamed in agony.

"You do not strike the breeder. She cannot breed if she is beaten, fool," Zach said reasonably, the hand that held Erik's fist squeezing slowly.

He was crushing Erik's fist. Sweat popped up on Erik's upper lip, his eyes widening.

"Please Master..." he wheedled.

"Please what, Intimate?" Zach asked coolly, as if he wasn't crushing a man's hand in his.

"I will not discipline the breeder."

"Why? Tell me why?"

"Because...because," his Adam's apple bobbed as he took a hard swallow, "I don't have the right," Erik finished in a miserable tone.

"You are not Vampire. You will not touch her again. If you do..." Zach opened his mouth wide and his fangs elongated, filling the space of his mouth. He leaned forward and put the tips delicately against the tender part of Erik's neck. "I will tear out the vein which pulses so strongly here."

My eyes unnervingly sought and found the pulse under those fangs where it beat frantically like a trapped animal.

"And worry at it like a canine with his favorite bone," Zach said with dark promise.

A terrible smell filled my nose and I looked down at the floor where a puddle was developing.

Erik had pissed himself.

Zach had made Erik clean his own pee off the floor while I watched.

I looked into his eyes as he watched me and Erik was bent over the task at hand.

"Very good. Now be about something else," Zach said, dismissing him neatly.

Erik scuttled away like a good submissive, backing away until his ass hit the door.

I was relieved to see him leave. My eyes flicked to Zach's and he had his obsidian stare trained on me. I couldn't read his expression. There should be a law against eyes that dark. Things were looking down, Erik gone, the *rogue* vampire alone in my room.

Trapped.

He eased down on the end of my bed. "I do not think we were properly introduced," he began.

"Oh, yeah, we were. Totally. Introduced," I said.

He smiled, the fangs flashing briefly in his pale face.

"I think you've got me mixed up with some other chick. I don't have anything special…you can just drop me off…wherever," I said with the straightest face I could manage.

Zach held up a hand. "Do not. We can smell what you are. Our intimate…"

I gave him a puzzled expression.

"The one whom you call Erik?" he cocked an eyebrow, confirming his identity.

I nodded.

"He is who we use during the daytime for interface." He shrugged.

"With who?" I asked.

"The humans, of course."

Oh.

"Not a really great choice. He's a big-time perv and he's violent. Obviously."

He smiled. "The dumb cattle are the ones easiest to manipulate."

There's the cattle term again. I scowled at him and he laughed. "What is the look for, Breeder? Do you hold your species in such high esteem? Truly?"

I really didn't but I wasn't going to let King Asshat know that.

I crossed my now-free arms underneath my breasts and scowled at him. "Us *mere humans* may not be up to your physical standards but we're not racing around bleeding everyone out. So, don't get on your high horse about how civil and superior you are. It isn't gonna wash with me."

The humor drained from his face as if it'd never been. He was suddenly so close to my face he was blurry. "And humans are so non-violent in their exploits. So restrained, so integrity-driven. Yes, *so worthy*. You are quite right, I was remiss."

He tucked a hair behind my ear and I flinched. "You have nothing to fear…"

"Rachel," I said.

The smile was back but just a small one, the fangs in hiding for the moment.

"Rachel…" he rolled my name on his tongue like sweet candy, "we need to speak about what has happened, your history, why you have come to be with the *rogue*."

"Forgive me, Zach, but I'm not buying. You kidnapped me from the 'good vamp'," I made airquotes and his frown deepened, "and then you, the bad vamp, came and took me with the help of your pervy sidekick creep, Erik. That makes you someone I don't need to trust." I threw my hands up in the air, landing them on my jean-clad thighs with a resounding smack.

"I am not the supposed 'bad vamp,' as you imply. Rather, our history is rich and varies from those vampires which held you in their breeding nest."

Yuck, I thought, shuddering.

⟋‾‾⟍

"Many years ago the Vampire and *rogue* were one." He made an elaborate gesture of dismissal, "But no more.

Vampire insist on breeding one Druid to two or more vampires. The *rogue* follow the human model; a single vampire to a Druid. They have left the ancient ways in their desperation for procreation."

I cocked a brow in disbelief. Forgive me if I was having a tough time coming to terms with their existence. If you add in the whole underlying faction angle…well, it was utterly unbelievable.

"I see that you disbelieve me," he stated.

"It *is* pretty unbelievable." He opened his mouth to reply, his fangs gleaming in the low light of the room but I rushed on, "I do believe that vampires exist, obviously. But you have to recognize that I didn't know who I was until yesterday. Then I was assaulted by their leader…"

"Alexander?" Zach said, his voice ringing with knowledge.

I nodded. "I supposedly have too much Druid blood to be put under 'compulsion', so he had to…" I gulped back the lump in my throat, the memory of his invasive fingers inside me one that I wouldn't forget any time soon.

Zach's expression darkened. "He forced you?"

My eyes met his black ones. "He tried, but Cole…" it was then that the mention of him brought back the events of the last ten hours. Why was I talking to him anyway? He took me from the one vampire that had actually given a shit. Now I sat here, unprotected, with the vampire that had tried to kidnap me in the glade. I crossed my arms, glaring at him.

"What?" he said, his eyes studying my face with glittering intensity.

"You took me from the one vampire that was actually protecting me! From you!"

"Is that what you think?" he asked in a low voice.

"Yes! After your stupid thug jerked my arm out of my socket, he healed me. *Cole did.* While you were too busy worrying about taking me to do it without violence." There, let him chew that and swallow the bitter pill of his choices. How could I believe he meant what he said when the way he had acted yesterday was in direct conflict?

"Of course he healed you. Any of us would have done the same. An injured breeder is not worth anything. How can Druids carry our seed if they are weak or hurting?"

I watched as his pupils dilated, nearly the same color as the iris and started shaking my head.

I backed up on the bed until my spine pressed against the cold metal of the headboard.

"Don't try your effed up mojo on me!"

He smiled, crawling across the bed until our faces were inches apart and I turned my head away, ignoring the pressure that pulsed from him. The need to look at him as he wished for me to. I felt heat flush through my system and he hadn't even touched me yet.

"It is true. Most Druids will respond well to compulsion. But some are most resistant. But I am special. That is why I have been chosen as the acquisition leader."

My eyes flicked to his and were instantly captured. It was different than with the Vampire...or Cole.

His eyes held heat and a question. I didn't move, I didn't breathe. My head told me he was the enemy, but as before with Cole, before I knew what they were, my body responded for me with a seductive whimper.

His face came closer, hovering briefly above mine. Then his lips pressed against mine, not harsh like I'd expected, but a languid and tender pull begun on my bottom lip. He sucked it in lightly, his tongue entering after his fangs had chewed the softness of my skin without breaking it. I groaned as his tongue moved inside my mouth, my ass sitting on my hands so they wouldn't touch him, and still he pecked and dove, exploring my mouth, his breath a male spice like early fall, cinnamon, apples and cider.

I was lost to it.

Still he didn't touch me with anything but his mouth. I gave up, kissing him back, my mouth moving with his, my hands still buried underneath my weight.

An inner resolve took hold over Zach, one palm cupping my face. It was so big against me it palmed most of my face and his touch electrified me. He put his other hand on the opposite side of my face, dragging me closer and I let him.

Still I held myself in check…until his hand wrapped around the slim column of my throat and his thumb began to move back and forth over the erratic pulse that beat there. I could feel his will pressing against mine and a dam broke. I sat up on my knees and he mirrored my movement, both of us facing each other, he inches taller, his mouth never breaking our kiss, his hand enveloping my throat. My hands became less rigid at my sides, they trembled with the effort not to touch him.

Finally, his mouth left mine and began to travel the hollows of my throat, his large hands moving to the small of my back and pressing our hips into an intimate kiss of flesh. He swept his tongue back and forth over that pulse then pulled back.

His hands latched onto my body were the only things that kept me from falling, I was that moved, that exhausted from resisting him.

"You will respond, eventually," and he smiled. His eyes traveling my flushed face and soft, ragged breathing.

I stared at him, feeling my resolve like the thinnest thread of willpower, ready to unravel. Once undone, I would collapse on him and I would become the aggressor.

"Take heart, Breeder, you are rare amongst your kind, as am I."

I took a shaky inhale and sat back on my heels, his hands falling away, leaving a trail of fire in their wake.

"What are you?" I whispered.

"I am your foil. I am the one that no Druid can withstand, no matter how pure the blood."

"Why?" I all but yelled. My misery was acute, knowing that at least I could choose with the others, tears burning the back of my eyelids in frustration.

"I am Druid as well."

2

Zach had left with a satisfied smirk on his face. The bomb dropped, he left me to deal with the debris.

I tried to sort through what he'd told me and why it should matter. The bottom line was I was in over my head, at a different place, still held against my will.

Then there was the problematic attraction thing. It's like no matter where I turned or how I intellectualized the whole shebang, those vamps had it goin' on. Zach was a problem but I could manipulate him. It was Erik that was the wild card. I'd seen the look he'd given me as he left my room.

He'd be back and I'd have to be ready.

I looked around the room, completely different from where I'd been held by Cole's group. It was an old house, the floor boards scarred with a hundred years of use, thick moldings wrapped the lone window and old door, a glass knob winked in the light cast from the window.

Strolling over to the window, I peered out at the yard below that wavered through the old glass like water running over its surface. *No fence*, I thought. Maybe escape would be easier.

Definitely their numbers were down, I thought with satisfaction, remembering the damage Cole had done to the other *rogue*. There was no love lost, I shuddered, remembering the one who'd hurt my shoulder. I rotated it tentatively, only a mild twinge proved the injury had ever occurred.

It made me think of Cole. What I'd told him. Guilt assailed me, I had told him I'd stay with him. It didn't matter how circumstances had brought us together. My former life was screwed beyond repair, I'd always be hunted. Better to be with someone that would defend me.

And I did care about him.

I sighed. My eyes caught sight of a pile of clothes on the very top of a free-standing wardrobe against the wall. I approached, watching my reflection as I came nearer, my face pale, purple smudges running underneath the blueness of my eyes. I looked like I'd been set on spin cycle in a washing machine.

Surveying the damage made me ache for a shower. Seeing another door, I reached out, the clothes in one hand and my other touching the solid glass knob. I turned the handle and pushed open the door into a small bathroom.

Maybe a shower would clear my head? *Better yet, maybe Cole would somehow find me…?* I thought uneasily as I set the clothing next to the claw foot tub positioned underneath a small window. Turning on the tap, I glanced at the water, thinking of Cole, pushing thoughts of Zach uneasily away....

Cole

Cole came awake with a bone crusher headache thumping like dull knives stabbing his temple. He lay astride Rachel's bed. It was up on end, he had thrown it against the window as an additional barrier against the dangerous orb of the sun. The bastard *rogue* had taken her shortly before dawn, it was the best he had managed.

Rage set in immediately. They had Rachel, and that damn coworker of hers, Erik, was a male without honor. He knew that Zach would not harm Rachel. But he would try to bond with her immediately, making it impossible for Cole to be with her, impossible for him to return to his kiss. With Rachel, he would have to share with his brethren. Without her, he would be condemned to a life of servitude for going against vampire law. There was not a single mate for a Druid. It had not always been so. Before their females became sterile, a male could choose who he wanted.

For love.

But no more. Now it was two to three males for one female. And finding a Druid with sufficient blood quantum was difficult. Nay, impossible. Rachel was very rare.

And Zach of the *rogue* had her.

Cole checked his breathing, forcing himself to breathe evenly. He must feed, then he would find her.

Somehow.

He would contact Nathan. He may have additional intel that would reveal a basic idea of the locale of the *rogue*.

Cole's eyes flicked to the clock, almost four p.m. But it was his body that told him night was nigh. Like all Vampire, he was finely-tuned to nightfall.

When that invisible switch flipped that told Cole night had fallen like a great obsidian blanket, he slipped out of Rachel's dwelling, snapping open his cell as he did.

He went west, where the car had taken the breeder.

Rachel.

Mine, he thought as he put on a burst of speed, scenting the air for prey.

For blood.

Nathan snapped the cell closed, a fine sheen of sweat on his upper lip, his eyes sliding to Alexander's.

"Does he believe you?"

"Why would he not?" Nathan answered.

Alexander walked toward him until their noses almost touched. He struggled against the three that held him, a hiss escaping his mouth.

"How dare you show aggression against me!" Alexander said, clenching his fist and jabbing Nathan in the solar plexus.

It momentarily stole Nathan's breath, but he had seen its advance and tightened up accordingly.

"Hold him, fool. You better have not uttered a code of some kind. I want that Reaper back here by nightfall, apprehended and subdued. He lost us that Druid and I will take it out of his hide."

Nathan accused, "You just want to breed with her yourself!" his breath coming shallowly from the hit.

Alexander's eyes narrowed. "No single vampire can have a Druid, you know that," his eyes betrayed his intent, his answer neatly deflecting the question.

"But you will bend the rules for what you want. And it was not Cole that allowed her to escape."

Alexander grabbed the back of Nathan's head and jerked him forward, his breath like death on him. "Then who was it?"

"I do not know! But it was Cole I came upon in the meadow. It was *he* who fought the *rogue* to reclaim her!"

The other vampires that held them shifted uneasily, their gazes lighting first upon Alexander then on Nathan.

"Lies!" Alexander said as his fists rained down upon Nathan, his blood spraying as the signet ring that Alexander wore tore and ripped at his flesh. The ruby in the ring flashed as his fist rose for a final blow and Nathan said in a fierce whisper through the gore in his mouth, "You do not deserve to lead."

The fist fell like a great meteorite, crashing into his skull and his vision wavered, growing dim, then gray.

Nathan knew no more.

Cole kept to the woods, hugging them closely, their shape masking his own. Long ago he had ascribed to the all-black wardrobe, instinctively understanding human's weak sight and all the camouflage that simple decision afforded him. He put himself against the rough bark of a Spruce tree, recounting the strange conversation he had with Nathan but minutes before.

"Nathan?"

"Yes, it is I."

Cole clutched the cell tighter, his acute hearing picking up on a subtle tension in Nathan's voice. He shifted his weight, thinking.

"Are you alone?"

"No."

Treading carefully.

"The rogue *have taken Rachel. They have a dangerous Intimate amongst them. He will have her at the first opportunity. Even now it may be too late."*

"Let us rendezvous."

"Is Alexander there?"

"Yes."

"You are going to give me the latest location of the rogue?*"*

"Yes."

"He will kill you if he finds you have helped me, Brother."

"I know."

Nathan told him the whereabouts of the rogue. *Where they suspected the* rogue *to be. He had also warned him by alerting him to their leader's presence.*

Subtly.

Alexander thought to reacquire Cole there. He might even think himself lucky enough to get Rachel back.

For himself. Make no mistake, that bastard Alexander wanted her for himself. She would give him what he was after: a Pureblood Druid.

The prophesy could be true. That a pureblood would be the one to allow vampires to walk during the day.

Daywalkers. A pure vampire and pure Druid mated could mean offspring that would free the Vampire from the night.

Free to live in the sun.

Free.

3

Zach's eyes bored into mine, his revelation a burning phrase that stood between us. The moment's ticked by as we stared at each other.

Finally I broke the silence, "I know that I can't hope for the life I had before. My cubicle job with a boss I hated, my friend Michelle...my cat. Gone," my voice broke on the words.

There was a grief in me for the familiar, the comfortable. It wasn't that my life had been so great before. It's that...it was what I knew. And now, with this stupid Druid blood in my veins, I was a sought-after commodity. That I'd even been comfortable enough with Cole proved that there was something to the biology of it all, whether or not I wanted to accept that reality. It was.

Zach looked at me as we sat facing each other, his hair, maybe red in his human existence, was a burnished copper, so different from Cole.

I watched his jaw tighten on his next words, "We are not without compassion. What do you think the *rogue* is about? We do not rape, we do not force unions with many," he said as he rolled his massive shoulders into a shrug. "But, we are not beyond the manipulation of our genetics for the betterment of all Vampire."

He clenched his eyes closed for a moment, the soot of his eyelashes like black lace against the paleness of his cheekbones. He opened them, momentarily dazzling me with the color of them...a shade of fine Merlot not found in nature.

"What about Erik? How does he fit into the picture? You may not be 'about' the things you just outlined, but he definitely is!" I crossed my arms beneath my breasts and stewed at him.

He smirked. "It is not so easy to procure willing humans. We are vulnerable during the daytime, we must trust who we can." He looked at me thoughtfully then said, "You are familiar with the phrase 'keep your friends close but your enemies closer'?" When I nodded he continued, "That is the caliber of what we choose. They long only for the superficial that we can provide, never caring for anything of real value. Erik," he said the name with some distaste, she noticed, "is but a tool. A tool in our acquisitions. It is the same for Cole's kiss." There was just the barest trace of sadness and I wondered at it. The origin of it a speculation constantly turning in my mind.

I opened my mouth to ask another question but he pressed a finger to my lips, the boiling heat of the contact going straight to my core. I gasped at the electricity of it and his eyes widened.

Nice to know it wasn't just me.

He snatched his finger back as if shocked but recovered, finally saying, "It is time to eat and for you to...become acquainted with your new surroundings."

I stood, unhappy that I had half the answers to twice the questions. Maybe, in the pie in the sky dream that I had, I would escape all of this and get so far away none of them would find me.

Zach led me through a series of strange hallways which reminded me of my aunt's house back east. When I was a child, I'd spend hot summers there and the halls turned and twisted, maze-like, until you'd get lost. These were like those. Doors at every turn, the place was ginormous, the biggest old house I'd ever been in. Finally, we reached the top of a staircase, the massive newel posts standing sentinel at the apex.

Zach turned his eyes to mine, the deepest color of red, I couldn't believe I'd thought they were black. "Watch your step, Rachel."

I smirked up at him, "Like I'll fall with you here. Precious-ass Druid that I am!" I laughed, thinking that I was already half-nuts for not being more scared or stunned at my situation. But the whole thing had a surreal quality to it, unbelievable I felt like I was going along with it, play-acting, no more.

I guess it would get serious when Zach put down the sexual hammer, wanting to bang me day and night, I thought with a smile. I'd be long-gone before that happened.

My hand trailed along the smooth wood of the hand-rail, Zach at my elbow. "Did you know Cole before you became *rogue*?" I asked, keeping his mind on questions instead of breeding me like a prize mule.

His face hardened and as we got to the last step, he took my elbow, frowning slightly, "You grow too thin, I can feel your bones."

I shrugged, gently removing my elbow from the big-ness of his hand. "It's been an exciting few days. I haven't had proper rest or food since before I was taken." I looked down, rolling my lip between my teeth, biting softly, trying not to let that sadness over the loss of my old life overtake me.

Zach turned me and put a hand underneath my chin, lifting my gaze to meet his. "It will all work out toward the best end, Rachel."

I held his gaze. "So you say."

We turned together on a sigh and headed to the large kitchen. My body needed more than physical sustenance.

I realized he'd never answered my question about Cole.

Cole

Cole let the body slide away from his grasp, licking the blood splatter around his mouth where he could. Drinking was a messy, yet necessary, task.

Cole gazed down at the already-cooling corpse at his feet and reveled in the luck of finding this one. Criminal as he was. Cole knew that he could find a victim that needed to pass into the Other by just cruising certain likely establishments. Like this one.

His gaze traveled to the neon sign. "Kodiak," it read. It was a known hang-out for the edgy young crowd that liked to dabble. Cole had found there was always enough of a certain element that wish to do wrong. They were normally in large enough numbers for Cole to satisfy his blood lust.

He toed the male's body like so much garbage. He'd been forcing a human female in the dark recesses of the alley, her glazed eyes and soft pleas for him to stop loud in Cole's acute hearing. The male never knew what hit him. The female's eyes widening was the only warning before he struck.

"Run!" Cole had hissed at her when she stood like a deer in the headlights. The body of the male thrashed underneath fangs that had sunk deep into its carotid artery. The sweet nectar of his neck pulsed directly into Cole's mouth. A burning highway of fuel he greedily gulped.

The female's eyes latched onto the sight, then found Cole's. Thinking faster than she had but moments before she scrambled away, falling twice as she raced to safety. *Cole was not usually viewed as a savior,* he thought with mirth. No matter that her assault in progress would have been a terrible ordeal and vile memory for years to come, his mouth pressed on the male as he succumbed to the blood letting would not be easily forgotten by her.

Or believed.

He turned on his heel, thinking that the *rogue* would be blamed for his hasty feeding. Already he could feel the blaze of power feeding an energy pipeline to his extremities. He lifted his nose to the air, scenting.

Catching something very faint, he spun in that direction.

He ran.

Zach made me laugh again and I was struck that I was laughing with my kidnapper. My smile faded, my appetite lessening.

He saw my expression and put hair that had fallen forward across my face behind my ear, his touch lingering at my temple.

I pulled back and his hand fell.

"I will not hurt you," Zach said.

I shrugged. "Having a hard time convincing myself of that with how things went in the glade…"

He nodded his head as if he understood. "Sometimes my comrades can be overzealous."

Overzealous my ass, I thought. My shoulder still throbbed if I moved it wrong. I unconsciously touched it and his eyes tracked my movement. As heat rose to my face I immediately scolded myself. I was not some blushing virgin to be intimidated by his touch. Still, it was so different than what I knew. And I was pretty inexperienced. I thought of Michelle and immediately set those thoughts aside. She was not here.

I wouldn't see her again. As soon as I got outta here, they'd go straight to my old digs and try to reacquire me.

Zach stood, pushing my half-eaten food away. "Does your shoulder still hurt you?"

I nodded silently as he moved closer, his hand a burning flame when it began to knead the skin that lay at the base of my neck.

"Here?" he asked in a whisper.

Oh my god, his hand felt so good, the smoothness of it rubbing and gently grabbing my flesh, stroking and bunching it at the junction where my neck connected to the injured shoulder. I couldn't help it, my head fell back and my lips parted. His hand tightened and drew me into the cradle of his body and my legs began to tremble as I felt his mouth a hair's breadth over mine. "Tell me not to kiss you and I will not."

The words stuck in my throat, I thought of my past life, Cole, whatever I could, but in the end, biology won out and with a soft groan I wound my arms around the vampire *rogue* who had kidnapped me from another, pressing my body against his.

With our bodies married hip to head he moved his mouth over mine, flattening his huge hands at the small of my back and pressing me against his hips. His shaft pressed against me and I involuntarily ground against it.

His sharp intake of breath startled me but he swung me into his arms and sprinted up the stairs as if the burden of me was light.

Things were moving too quickly and I struggled, out of breath and he fell on me as I became pinned beneath him. He clasped my wrists and held them over my head, blazing a trail of hot kisses from my mouth then pecking his way down to my nipple. Aggressively sucking it through my thin tee, it hardened and became a stiff pebble of aroused flesh in his mouth and I groaned at the assault. As his fangs maneuvered around the delicate area, the barest thread that led from my nipple to my core throbbed with each pull of his mouth, each suckling. I was soon panting and out of breath. My resolve weakened, my resistance, gone.

He spread my legs and tore off my jeans with a jerk. I began to close them when he pressed them open again. I struggled against his hands. "No…I'm not ready for this…"

His eyes met mine, my fingers driven into his hair and straining to keep his head away from my pussy. Which in no time he'd find was soaking wet from his foreplay. What defense would I have then?

"I but wish to taste you, give you pleasure. I do not ask for sex yet."

I dropped my head back, beaten.

He dipped his head down, moving a finger along the lace of the panties I wore. Back and forth that blunt finger worked until I was about nuts. Just as I thought I'd beg for him to stop or do more, he slid my panties to the side and planted the flat of his tongue on my clit. My body shuddered and I moved the slightest bit against his seeking mouth, all the while feeling ashamed at my behavior. I meant to leave, not lie here, legs spread, shoving my pussy in a vampire's face. But oh...what he did to me. Zach knew female anatomy and lifted his head to ask me what I liked.

"Do you like my tongue like this?" he asked as he stabbed it inside my wet hole. My hips jumped and he put a forearm down on my belly to hold me in place as he fucked me with his tongue.

"Tell me you like it," he purred against my ripe opening and the vibration of his voice reverberated against me as I got closer to orgasm. A small part of me felt like I should say *no, get away*...something. But my blood roared to meet his in a heated call I couldn't ignore. I didn't know him, but my blood did. He felt the same, groaning as he licked and sucked along my delicate folds of flesh.

When I felt his finger enter me I arched my back and grabbed his copper hair again, jerking his face off me even as his fingers dove in and out of my channel, pulling rhythmically, getting me closer to that delicious explosion I was helpless to stop.

"Please..." I began.

"Please what?" he murmured. My hands fisted in his hair did nothing to stop his motions. If he'd wanted to go down on me again he could have. His eyes were deep and drowning obsidian pools, liquid and heated.

"Please more," he whispered. I nodded even as my brain said *no*.

I nodded yes.

He plunged his mouth into my pussy and tore his hands out of me and shoved them underneath the small of my back, lifting my hips to get better access to my pussy. Spreading me wide, he rubbed his face back and forth across my sensitive skin and with a final plunge of his tongue I orgasmed. In his face.

Again and again.

We lay together afterward, Zach spooning me from behind as I cried my frustration into his muscular arm.

"What is it? Did I not pleasure you?" he asked, tenderly kissing the side of my face while the tears soaked him.

"You did! That's not the point!" I wailed.

"What is wrong then?"

"I am not like...that. I don't do those things with everyone, anyone."

"It is not your fault. Think of it as a biological imperative. You are drawn to us sexually. It was what you were made to do. Females of Druid blood are the only humans with whom we may breed. It is true that we can have sex with any human female."

The caveat hung in the air.

I turned to look at him. "But what?"

He looked a little embarrassed and that was saying something. None of the vamps I met seemed to lack confidence.

"It is always pleasurable but it is so much more with a breeder. And a pureblood?" His eyebrows shot up and he sighed, dipping his head into the crook of my neck. "With a human female, we wish only to relieve our needs, take what is necessary."

I scowled at him and he laughed. "It is true, I dare say. But with the Druid, it is our biological imperative to give pleasure. It is in the fabric of our very design."

His lips lay a trail on my neck, then went to my collarbone and as he sat up, he moved to the dip at my waist. Finally, he landed at my hip, his lips spreading and kissing a hot circle where the bone met the roundness of the side.

"Stop," I whispered, the heat flaring like an ember brought to life between us.

His eyes rolled to mine and in one fluid motion he carried me to the bath, giving the tap a viscous jerk to the left. The water sprayed out, steaming as it landed in the porcelain. His eyes grew dark as he said, "I have patience aplenty. But I do mean to have you. And do not think that Cole does not seek you even now."

I looked around, naked in his arms, thinking Cole would come through a crevice in the house.

His eyes lightened and he chuckled. "He does not come through walls, even him."

I looked into Zach's eyes. "We have shared this together, you know."

I watched his face as the knowledge that Cole had tasted me also cloaked him. His expression grew fierce.

He drew me closer and said, "Has he buried his flesh in yours, Breeder?"

He scared me and the truth flew out of my mouth, "No!"

He relaxed his hold on me. "I will not rape you. But, know this, if I can have you when you are fertile, I may be able to bond you to me and me only, then Cole would be out of the race for you as mate."

Wow, this was looking bad. I couldn't even think of when I had my period last or anything. The bonding thing seemed pretty permanent.

"Am I...?"

He shook his head. "No...but soon." He turned the spigot off and placed me in the tub slowly, the almost hot water moving in around me like a wet shroud of warmth.

He pinched one of my nipples and I shivered underneath his touch. My core blossomed for him, opening like a wet and ripe flower. My lip trembled. I was hating how weak I was to the vampires.

I had to get out of here. But first I had a question.

He saw it on my face. "What do you wish to ask?"

"So...I'll just lay there and spread my legs for any vampire because of having Druid blood? I have no protection against any of you?" A hot tear rolled out of my eye. I didn't care that he said it wasn't rape. I knew what I didn't want intellectually but my body chose for me.

Therefore, zero choice.

Zach shook his head. "No, vampires with Druid blood, Reapers. Those two groups. Lowly Vampire, no. We would, none of us, ever waste a Druid on degenerate Vampire stock. And," he swiped the tears on my face away with the gentlest of strokes, "your blood knows which to choose. Those reactions you had to me while I..." a hot blush rode to my face and he sucked in his breath, watching that enticing blood bloom underneath the surface of my skin. He took a shuddering exhale and began again, "Were it me to take you. Take you then. Your blood knows which it calls to most. It will decide for you."

"What of rape?" I asked, thinking of that vampire that had nearly torn my arm off.

He shrugged. "It can happen. Any vampire will want you more than any other female, vampire females included. Our blood knows which female will ripen when she takes our seed within her body."

I slid down into the tub. I thought about being raped by one of them. It wasn't something I'd survive. I knew it.

He saw my barely concealed fear and spoke again, "You are well guarded, a treasure. The *rogue* understand your importance very well. Without the Druid, we will be no more." He spread his hands wide as if defeated. "We need you, you are too important. Only the derelict would assault a Druid and live to tell about it."

"Has it happened?"

He nodded, expression somber. "It has."

"What...what happened?"

Zach didn't answer immediately, but slid a long, tapered finger along the rolled rim of the tub. Finally he looked up, his wine-colored eyes boring into mine. "He was rough with her...he shattered her pelvis and broke her jaw."

I gasped in a breath, covering my mouth, my eyes widening.

"Why would he hurt her?"

"He held her face and used a hand on her hip to hold her still while he…" his eyes flicked to mine and when he saw I understood he went on, "We were unable to save her."

"What about him!" I cried, the water lapping the edges of the tub with my movement.

He smiled. It wasn't a smile of pleasure but one of retribution. "The *rogue* pulled him apart while his heart still beat. The Druid female watched even as her life bled out of her," he finished softly.

I realized he cared. He had cared about the female.

"Who was she? Who was she to you…?"

His eyes never left hers.

"My sister."

Cole

Cole slowed his run to a jog. He was very near the coordinates that Nathan had given him but dawn was close. He must find shelter and resume his search, make it finer.

Looking around he spied a heap of rocks. After exploring it thoroughly, he saw that it was but a covering for an old mine shaft, plentiful in this area. They thought nothing of blasting whatever piece of the environment would yield a resource of value to exploit. Especially in the era he was most familiar with, post WWII. That is when he had been turned.

And needed for his task. The harvest of Druids.

There were few Reapers. Many recruited, few chosen. There was a certain component for successful acquisition. He had done very well. Alexander had been pleased.

Until Rachel.

He burrowed under the earth, dreamless sleep sucking him under, thoughts of finding her in the next twenty-four hours foremost on his mind.

Nathan paced back and forth in his cell, already his face healing from the damage Alexander had meted out through his low Vampire. Drones, really. But they were still effective when it was one against four. There was no way to warn Cole. They would drag him out to the place he had been forced to reveal. It was the true coordinates. Although the *rogue* was near, they would kill Cole. They would reacquire the Druid breeder, forcing her to breed with at least three of the Reapers. Their mission was clear.

He remembered Rachel's fire. The taste of her blood, the feel of her skin beneath his fingers. It was better that Cole have her than he. He had a debt to his warrior friend, and he intended to keep it.

I stared at him after that proclamation. I didn't know what to say but said what I could, "I'm so sorry."

"It has been many years," he looked up at me sharply and continued, "but I have not forgotten the lesson taught therein."

"And what was that?" I asked softly, beginning to make a lather with shampoo for my hair, so glad to be in a position of getting clean my modesty at his intimate presence didn't faze me. Even if the subject discussed was so sad.

"He was her guard. She had become close to him. When he made an advance, she thought nothing of it, but when she realized it was not a casual overture..."

"What?" I asked, my hair a soapy turban on my head.

"She tried to break away, but he was consumed by blood lust and lust for her body, of course. She struggled and he broke her body to keep her still. It was not until we pulled him off that he realized that in his fervor to have her, he had killed her."

"What was her name, Zach?" The soap stilled in my slick hands.

He bent over the tub, taking the soap from me and dipping it beneath the steaming water then lathering. He began to move the soap over my bare back and I almost moaned with pleasure. Hands so strong, capable of so much damage, moving softly over my body.

I thought he would not answer but when he was behind me he said, "Jasmine."

"Like the flower," I clarified.

I could almost feel him nod, although no sound escaped his lips.

He moved around my body and I let him, our silence had its own rhythm. He washed my toes, then my ankles, when he reached my sweet spot he gently lathered and took his time, moving a finger along the folds and swirling the soap and water around it with an erotic pull. It was exquisite torture and he knew it. Just when I thought I would scream from the sexual tension, he moved on, working his way up my body, ending with a gentle kiss on my lips.

"I will not let it end like it did for my sister...with you."

He had not forgotten what we'd been talking about, he had just taken a break from the gravity of it all.

I rinsed the soap off my body and he stood, a plush towel in his arms. He opened it for me and I stepped out of the tub and into the towel.

Into his arms.

Cole

C ole's eyes snapped open. Disorientation slipped away on the wind. He could feel the pressure of the moon, on the wane but still ripe, an insistent pressure against his mind. Velvet reassurance that night had fallen. He thought briefly of feeding, then dismissed it. He would have to press forward, getting by on his last feed.

He exited the old mining shaft and scented the air around him, stretching his limbs, feeling himself again after the horrible sedative that human had shot him with.

He would die. Cole remembered that Rachel had seemed to know the human. He did not like knowing that she was possibly in his care. He had watched her quite closely and in the brief time that it had taken the *rogue* to acquire her he was more anxious about the Intimate's involvement than the *rogue*. The other may damage her. Zach of the *rogue* would not.

He sighed. Finally, after a few minutes of tracking, he caught the slightest trace of her fragrance, vaguely like fruit and spice.

He ran toward it.

The scent.

Rachel.

Nathan had been released, healing from the beating he had received at his leader's fist. He had never been a supporter of Alexander. But it was his rage over losing a breeder that he wished for himself that had caused him to become unhinged, beating one of his best Reapers because she was not within his grasp. And Nathan had abetted her escape. Not initially, but letting Cole go and not alerting the coven of Rachel's escape and Nathan taking her had been an unpardonable error.

He had been punished. Now, starvation and the need to feed was a burning blood lust in his body, every nerve ending on fire. He struggled outside, on the prowl for the first poor soul that he could find.

Alexander had all but thrown him outside the coven doors. Nathan remembered his directive, "Do not return until you have something worthy of this coven. A Druid, Reaper. Keep in mind what we have lost, what we may never have. That the rogue *now take pleasure in."*

Nathan had gone. Alexander's resentment tasted like bitter ash upon his tongue.

He roamed the back alleys, getting closer to the university campus. Normally, he would have cruised the seedier sections of town, finding a male to ravage, one that was about to commit nefarious deeds. That is exactly what he preferred. Now he would be forced to bleed a female while burying his shaft to the hilt inside of her. Alexander had thrown him out and made many vulnerable because of his blood lust. It had turned into a beast of its own, now sexual need combined inexorably with the blood lust.

Neither easily separated.

His ears pricked at the sound of feminine voices coming his way. Two females, his nose told him. His blood roared to be satiated. He came out of the alleyway into full view of the females, his huge body tense and ready to spring.

Holly laughed at what Jill said, throwing her scarf around her neck. Damn thing kept coming forward. The smile melted off Holly's face as she watched Jill's face fall, filling with fear.

What the hell? Holly whipped her head in the direction Jill was staring, her feet pegged to the ground and a dazed expression on her stunned face.

In front of Holly stood the biggest man she had ever laid eyes on. Forget WWE, this guy made them look puny.

Holly's heart raced, he stood stock-still, all black menace and grace. He was coming at them in a jog, intent on his face.

Holly wasn't gonna stick around to see what he planned. She screamed at Jill, "Run!"

Holly turned and in one moment, her scarf that she had secured more tightly around her neck was the thing he used to jerk her back against him.

Ah hell, she thought, her vision growing dim, as the scarf became a noose.

Holly collapsed against Nathan, her airway constricted by the scarf, fear choking her into unconsciousness.

Jill fought him as he dragged her off into the alley. The other human female was tucked safely underneath his arm, she was so small it was simple.

Too simple, really.

He set the unconscious female down on the ground, careful not to let her hit her head as the other kicked and fought, screaming.

Nathan could not have that. He looked into her eyes. "Be silent."

She stopped mid-scream. His pupils dilated and he licked his lips, the fragrance of her blood enticing a clamor he could not deny.

He did not need to kill this one. After all, he had two.

He gave the command, the chill of the air making fog of his breath, "Spread your legs, female."

Jill did, her mind roaring to stop, her body mechanically doing what he asked.

He tore off her tights that she wore for warmth underneath her skirt and she felt his fingers prob the hot recesses of her pussy. Missing nothing he pushed a finger inside her and a moan escaped.

Nathan smiled, the human females were so easy. He just willed their compliance and they were instantly aroused. Spread and ready for the vampires use. He pumped his fingers inside the female until her pussy was slick with her honey and looking around for others, seeing the alley was empty, he positioned his throbbing shaft above her. Pressing inside her he rocked forward then back, his face a mask of tenseness, relief not in sight yet. The female moved her hips up to capture his rod, forcing herself higher upon him.

He tore her blouse open, exposing her throat, the tearing material the only sound in the alley. Ice dripped from the hot roofs in the background while he rutted on top of her. He tensed then said, very close to release, "Turn your head." She did, even as she rose to meet his hard thrusts. He was burying himself to the root inside her, she was taking all his hard length inside. *She would be very sore tomorrow*, he thought, shoving himself in her tight snatch harder. As he fought orgasm just a moment longer, Nathan felt his fangs elongate, readying him for ejaculation.

They punched out of his mouth and the hand he had cupped underneath the female's neck forced her close to his face as he struck, his cock spurting hot jets of seed deep inside her slick channel as his fangs penetrated the tender flesh of her throat.

He orgasmed and bled her simultaneously. Her body writhed underneath him, even as she slipped into unconsciousness, her pussy milked him, throbbing around him like a pulsating fist. He threw his head back, blood dripping from his fangs. With a groan he pulled out of the female. He arranged her clothes and licked the wounds he had made. He did not like killing females. It had been a near thing because his control was precarious at best.

He looked around the alley, the female in his arms. Seeing the first door he could find, a quick glance at the second female, laying there. He frowned, the cold of the ground would be leeching through her clothing. Time to hurry. He kicked open the door and laid the female he had used inside the door of the warm dwelling.

Good. He arranged her so when she awoke she would not be vulnerable.

Nathan felt better. He did not like to use the human females but he could not impregnate them and that one had been no virgin, her pussy accepting his girth like she was meant for it, key to lock. He smiled, moving toward the other female.

Her smell assaulted him.

He stopped in his tracks. How he had missed it when it was right underneath his nose he did not know. But the siege of blood lust had been upon him when he captured and bled the first victim he had found.

The other female was Druid. He could smell it like a fine wine on his tongue. He sprinted to her side, lifting her off the cold ground. Her stillness worried him. He cocked his head, listening for her heartbeat.

It was strong, she lived. He cradled her small body against him and sprinted for a location of privacy.

As he passed underneath a streetlight he caught sight of her face and stopped in his tracks. The female looked exactly like another Druid.

Exactly.

Rachel.

He had Rachel.

Holly

Holly came awake and her vision was instantly filled by a huge form, his silhouette overwhelming her.

The memories of the attack flooded her mind in a slipping sludge and she screamed, her voice box going hoarse with it. A large, cold hand covered her mouth, the size so large it cupped her face. Her scream died against his flesh.

She looked up at him, her bladder clenching uncomfortably and knew she would die. Instinctively, Holly knew that they were alone, Jill gone. Fat tears ran down her face. She would die here with a lunatic. He might do things to her. Holly thought of how young she was, inexperienced. She was just a freshman in college.

A virgin. Her wide blue eyes flicked to his, glittering marbles of deep inky black fire stared back.

Then he spoke, "Be still. I mean you no harm, Druid."

Holly listened in confusion. What was a Druid? She was a woman, she didn't know what he was talking about. And she didn't believe him on the no harm thing, either.

"If I remove my hand, will you stay quiet?" his brows lifted.

She nodded her head. He was huge. If he wanted to subdue her, he sure could.

He slowly lifted his palm away and sat crouched back, ready. She crawled away until her back met something solid.

They regarded each other and after a moment he said, "You are safe with me."

Holly shook her head and asked, "Where's Jill?"

His eyes shifted away then came back to her gaze. "She is safe."

Holly's voice trembled and she asked, "What are you going to do with me?"

Nathan thought about softening the blow but thought that her knowing may secure her compliance...or not. "Breed you. I will breed you."

Holly was stunned into silence. Then she looked at him, her eyes taking in everything. There was something other-worldly about him. His eyes had looked black but with the moonlight coming through a dirty pane of glass they had silvered, reflective in the strange bluish-white light.

"What are you?" she whispered, her voice quaking.

"I am a Reaper," he said, his eyes never leaving hers.

"What...what is that?"

"I am Vampire," Nathan said.

Holly made a move to leap from her perch and he was there in a blur of gray, her eyes unable to track his speed.

Her breath came in a hitching gasp and he held her while she squirmed against him, his shaft growing against her with her movements, arousing him.

"Please…" Holly begged, "please don't rape me."

Nathan kept her against him and as she struggled to get away, he captured her chin and easily forced her gaze to lock with his. "I did not say I would rape you."

Holly stopped struggling, his erection straining between them. "If you aren't going to rape me then what are you going to do?"

Nathan smiled, his path clear. "Keep you, protect you…breed you. Maybe, eventually, you will come to care for me."

Holly sagged in his huge arms, she felt the heat climb her body beginning at her feet and knew that she was in the first stage of shock.

Being captured by a mythological vampire that wanted to have babies with her would do it.

Nathan gathered the small Druid in his arms as she fainted for the second time that night. He clasped her against his chest protectively and studied her face. He had been wrong. She was not the Druid that Cole had rescued. But she was a relation. Of that he had no doubt.

Their features were uncannily similar, except for the size. This Druid was built like a doll, and very young.

Untried.

He would be her first.

Very soon.

I stretched my arms above me, feeling Zach beside me. He had not pressed me for more, sensing my conflicting feelings about Cole, about my circumstances, about my internal emotions of escape. I didn't know what to think.

What to do.

If I escaped I would have to find shelter, with not a cent. I sighed and Zach's eyes snapped open, instantly alert and ready.

For anything.

He wrapped a muscular arm around me and pulled me close, kissing me softly and I stiffened. Too confused to even pretend to know what to do.

He pulled away with a frown. "You will warm to me eventually," he said.

Zach got out of the bed and dressed, his ass clenching and flexing deliciously as he put on some soft pants and turned, catching me admiring him.

I watched as his cock grew in the pants and met his gaze uneasily.

"Do not worry, we will go at your pace. But my body grows impatient. And that, I cannot help."

With a sigh, he threw on a tight T-shirt and strode to the door. His hand clenched the door frame until the knuckles bled white. "I will return in one half-hour to escort you for breakfast."

I looked at the night sky out the window. "But it's…"

He nodded. "It is breakfast for us. It will be something you grow accustomed to as well." His face grew wistful. "Maybe one day, the night will not be my prison."

I pulled the sheets up to my chin.

Because of me. The Druid mates could supposedly tolerate daylight. Because of me. Because of my blood.

He smiled, seeing my internal machinations and strode out the door.

I exhaled in a rush, my thoughts a distracted tangle of two men, my life and escape.

I began to dress when I heard the doorknob rattle. *What was he doing back so soon,* I wondered? He'd said one half-hour.

I put my pants in front of me, shielding the view of my panties. My bra was half exposed through the shirt I'd thrown on and I met Erik's hungry gaze.

Oh fuck, I lamented and turned to run, slamming the bathroom door behind me. I turned the lock just as his shoulder slammed into it, the wood giving and splintering against the lock.

He came through the door, slamming it against the wall and I ran behind the tub, my hair still damp from the bath chilling against my skin, damp with stress and fright.

"Get over here you uppity bitch!" he hissed at me, his hands balled into fists. "You're gonna give me what I need and that stupid vamp isn't around to stop me." He grabbed his crotch with one hand and my stomach fell. All this talk of not raping Druids and how important they were to the Vampires and this loser human was going to rape me. It didn't matter how precious I was to them, he didn't care. I was just another woman to abuse to him. My importance to them became lost in the face of his perversion.

Cole

Cole came upon the house easily enough. The scent of the *rogue* was thick in his nostrils. The lair was within reach. But he mustn't just charge in. There would be too many guards. He would watch and see the perfect time to infiltrate their hideaway. He looked up at the place, maybe at one time an old hospital from the war, built stout and large, it looked like it was the right size to hold a coven the size of the *rogue.*

Cole chose his perch carefully and began his grim watch. All the while knowing that Rachel was within those walls. His nose told him so.

It also told him she was near her fertile time.

He sat for a moment or two and heard a high keening noise. It was a sound that made him leap to his feet. He would know it anywhere.

The sound of a female in distress and under attack.

He moved with a speed he did not know he possessed.

I struck Erik in the face with the back brush that was located beside the tub I'd just relaxed in. His nose opened cooperatively and blood fountained out of it like a fire hydrant.

He swung with his body and backhanded me, sending me careening into the wall. My head struck first and I saw stars. He was on me that fast, wrapping his hand in my long hair and crushing his mouth to mine, blood and spit mixed in with his assault. He dragged my panties down and grabbed my sex roughly, hurting me. I moaned in pain with the last little bit of consciousness I had as I clamped down on his lip with my teeth, nearly meeting them together. He howled, staggering backward and I slid down the wall until my bare butt hit the cold tile, panties at my ankles. My bell had been rung by the blow and I didn't have the strength to pull them up.

Even when Cole blasted through the window I didn't stir. It couldn't be him...he was, I couldn't think where he was, glass spraying in a brittle rain all around me.

"Rachel!" he roared, coming at me.

I pointed to Erik thinking thickly that he needed to have his ass taken care of. Forget me for the moment. Cole turned to where I pointed and in a spinning leap he was on Erik who mewled for mercy underneath him.

Too late.

Cole plunged his fangs into his large throat and tore out his esophagus. I felt my head go light and threw it between my knees. It spun when I closed my eyes, a vision of Erik's breathing tube like a grotesque worm on the tile, his vile blood spilling everywhere.

Then Cole was before me, gently lifting my face to meet his. The first words out of his mouth were, "Has he had you?"

I began to cry and he shook me gently. "Has he?" he asked softly, his eyes belying the tenderness of his voice.

I shook my head. *He'd been very close to having me,* I thought dismally, but by some stroke of luck they hadn't. Probably because Zach was good. Somehow, he was Vampire but he was a good vampire.

I began to laugh and Cole looked at me, puzzled. I realized that getting hysterical was not good.

Didn't matter, I couldn't stop laughing then the laughter turned to sobs. It wasn't until the other *rogue* filled the doorway and I met Zach's eyes that I stopped crying. Cole pulled my panties up one handed, my dizziness slowing the awkward maneuver to a snail's pace.

Cole jerked Rachel behind him, his anger beating a staccato rhythm in his temple. His vision of Rachel half naked and her face bearing the mark of a fist made him want to kill everything in sight. He took in the human, his windpipe laying beside him and wished with a vicious lust he could have beat him with it had he still been alive.

Zach also took in the scene. Rachel had been beaten and his Intimate dispatched.

His eyes shifted to hers and he felt a remorse more profound than any he had ever known. He had tough choices to make. Not the least of which was: if he harmed Cole, without knowing more of her relationship with him, would she ever mate with him? Yet, if he did not get rid of the primary competition for her affection, all was lost.

Zach smiled coolly at Cole. "I see thanks are in order, Reaper."

Cole met his eyes, Rachel a trembling presence behind him. "I thought that you would take better care of a Druid of this purity," Cole responded. Rachel saw Zach's eyes flinch. "Yet, here she was, ready to be savaged by a human. Common livestock," he enunciated with derision, his palm indicating Erik.

Zach's eyes narrowed. "I was negligent. Leaving him to guard her when I knew there was a disobedient streak with that one." He looked at Rachel. "I am sorry that I left you unprotected with him."

Rachel didn't know what to think. They were a violent people, race, whatever.

It was a stalemate. She knew that Cole would fight for her. But as she looked at Zach, the stern lines of his face, the determination etched there said the same.

They squared off. Cole moving forward.

Rachel clenched her eyes together, the wind from the broken window chilling her skin into a riot of gooseflesh.

A *rogue* rushed into the room, causing both vampires to swivel into a defensive crouch toward him.

"Captain!" Zach straightened, focusing one eye on the newcomer and one on Cole.

Cole was honorable, he would not attack another vampire unawares.

"What?" His eyes narrowed on the *rogue*, who shifted in nervousness but said, "There is another on the grounds."

Cole's eyebrows shot up and, picking up Rachel to avoid the shards of broken glass on the floor, he traveled to the window, scenting.

He would recognize that fragrance anywhere, Druid. His nostrils flared and he picked up another. A familiar scent wafted on the wind, hitting his acute network of olfactory senses. All of them ringing together, matching the signature to the vampire.

Nathan had come.

And with him, another Druid.

7

Holly was cold. The mammoth creature by her side did not generate a lot of body heat and between being terrified of the next five minutes and feeling dazed because of fainting she just wanted to check out on reality. It was impossible for her to believe that just three short hours ago she and Jill had been walking back from study group. A boring thing, more of an excuse to get together and gossip about guys and the latest scandal than to get any practical work done.

She was too much of a coward to ask about Jill. She didn't know if she *wanted* to know. It was pretty daunting just holding her own with the male that was named Nathan. At least that's what he called himself. Then he'd told her that he'd caught the "scent" of his buddy, Cole.

Of course, Holly thought, he hadn't called him his buddy, but "comrade." He spoke really weird. Holly couldn't put her finger on it but he sounded a little like that hot guy out of the old movie, *Kate and Leopold.* Her initial fear had quieted. Holly was innately practical and knew that if she wanted to get away from this freak that she'd have to bide her time. She had to admit though, when he wasn't looming over the top of her and talking about breeding all the time he had a real pull on her.

Like a magnet.

It was a little scary. She'd felt him up against her when she struggled and he was built huge. She didn't want *that* inside her. She wanted her first time to be with someone she loved, not some crazy guy that sucked people's blood. She felt a hysterical bubble of laughter well up inside her and recognized, on some level, she was in a state of shock.

She stood next to Nathan. He looked down at her dark head and pulled her in closer to his side for warmth.

For protection

Nathan stood underneath a great sweep of trees, the small Druid pressed to his side, his weapons cold comfort against his body, necessary bulges underneath his lightweight clothing.

Vampires were naturally impervious to the cold.

Looking up at the old building he saw a curtain like a gauzy flag waving out of the shattered pane, loud voices coming from inside. His sensitive hearing picked up and triangulated the position of a familiar voice.

Cole.

He would know what to do. Together, they could escape. There would be a chance with the women. He would not return to Alexander's coven. There the Druid virgin would be passed around like meat, their only motivation to impregnate her and get their coveted vampires that walked in daylight. As long as Nathan had breath in his body, he would not let that be her end.

He pressed her closer while he made his way toward the structure.

Cole stepped away from the window, his vision picking up Nathan with a Druid clutched under his side. She looked like a girl, not a woman. Cole frowned.

I didn't see what Cole was looking at but he turned with purpose. "Do not follow me. Leave this alone, *rogue*. Leave Rachel alone," he commanded.

Zach narrowed his eyes as Cole backed us toward the open window. "I cannot," he said softly and rushed Cole in a blur of speed.

Cole pushed himself backward with one arm pressing against me as we fell backward out the window, the cold air hitting me like a punch in the gut. He did a spin midair that made me want to throw up and landed on his feet, scooping me against him as he fell.

Zach barreled into the two of us and my body slipped out of Cole's grasp and I tumbled into the snow, my bare legs instantly soaked and freezing.

I wouldn't last long in this weather without proper clothing.

The vampires went at each other in a flurry of hands. Too fast for me to track, the meaty sounds of flesh connecting with flesh were the only noises in a forest surrounding a building gone silent except for them.

The remaining *rogue* poured out through the door, circling the fighting vampires cautiously.

I stood on shaky legs. My feet were screaming with pain in the cold snow, my body starting to shiver, teeth chattering. Behind me I heard a small noise. Turning away from the fighting I saw a girl that looked about nineteen. Even in the gloom I could see we could have been sisters. She looked so much like me I gasped in surprise.

Holly looked at a tallish woman in nothing but panties, bra, and half a ripped blouse, while two huge men beat the snot out of each other behind her, blood splattering the snow like oil flung, the blackness pockmarking the whiteness.

She tried to leave Nathan and go to the other woman but he held her. Holly felt immediately connected with her. Her chest tightened uncomfortably.

I came toward the girl and the…Reaper. I could definitely tell what he was. I remembered him from the meadow.

"Nathan?" I asked. And suddenly Zach and Cole were beside me, their ragged breathing and beaten faces tense.

Nathan hissed and stepped in front of the young Druid while Cole tried to tear me away from Zach.

I found myself wanting to sleep. The beginnings of hypothermia were setting in.

Cole gave me a worried glance and picked me up where I stood.

Zach said, his mouth bloody, "The *rogue* will not let you take her, Reaper."

Holly looked at the two vampires. Because that was what they were, their fangs sprung and dark, wearing the blood of each other. The one that was slightly bigger held the woman in his arms, cradling her. Her hands and feet were turning an alarming shade of blue.

Holly looked around Nathan, his big body blocking hers and met the stare of the male with silver eyes.

Something clicked inside Holly like a hammer on a gun drawn and ready to strike. It reverberated in her chest, a bell struck.

Zach looked at the small female before him, pressed up against the Reaper that claimed her as protector and felt something integral in his chest slide into place as if it had been waiting for this moment to come together. His body righted itself.

Holly moved toward him before she realized she was and Nathan roared, "No!" in a bellowing wail, rushing Zach.

Cole backed up, realizing how the tide had turned.

A true mate had been imprinted upon. It was the *rogue* and the new Druid. They were meant to be together.

A true mating pair. A thing of legend.

Cole would have to stop Nathan. He looked down at Rachel, her warmth perilously slipping away. She would die if he could not attend to her.

Holly ran for the man in front of her. Needing to touch him, connect to him, as if he was food and she was starving. She didn't question the instinct, but acted on it like a compulsion. Her feet propelled her forward into the dark, into the arms of a vampire.

He was the one for her.

Zach saw the girl come for him and he rushed forward to meet her even as he saw a group of vampires enter the clearing.

Alexander entered the clearing with his finest contingent of Reapers. They had scented the Druids to these coordinates. The very location they knew to be a *rogue* coven.

He saw Nathan and Cole, a *rogue* and the two Druids. One was Rachel. His mouth salivated as he thought of his fingers buried in her core and what he almost had within his grasp. Shoving his lust away with an effort he looked at the other breeder, who bore a startling likeness to Rachel. He compared the two. Then something strange happened. The young Druid rushed the *rogue* and leapt onto him, causing him to stagger back, the moonlight revealing wounds that had been inflicted by fists. He knew that damage. His eyes shifted to Cole, who was holding a shivering and comatose Rachel. His jacket was wrapped around her to conserve her body heat.

Why she was in her underthings remained a mystery. She had better not have been tried, he thought, signaling the Reapers to flank the group.

Cole brought Rachel in closer to his body and with one arm put a restraining palm on Nathan.

"No!" Cole yelled, straining against Nathan's charge. Nathan whipped his head around to Cole and said, "She is mine! I found her, she is not for the *rogue*!" His eyes were wild and pinned on Holly.

"Look with eyes not consumed by lust!" Cole shouted. "They are a true, mated pair."

Holly slammed into Zach and got up on her tiptoes and began to kiss him, touch him. The blood on his face was inconsequential to her. She could not get close enough to him. He groaned into her mouth and wrapped her up in his arms, picking her up against him, even as his eyes took in the leader of their enemy coven.

Zach felt every protective instinct he possessed fire up and come together into a pure rage, focused at the threat at hand. He watched the Reapers spread out and surround their group.

He turned with the young Druid in his arms, assessing where his vampires were and saw that the match was even, their bodies already poised for battle.

He let the girl slide down his front and felt a loss at their parting.

Holly whimpered to the man that held her and clung to him. She knew that she shouldn't feel like she did but every fiber of her being screamed for him.

Zach stroked her hair, pressing her face against his chest, hissing at the newcomers.

His fangs dripped toxic venom onto the snow.

Alexander entered the deepest part of the clearing, taking in the two Reapers that appeared weary, the *rogue* that had been beaten and had all the protective hallmarks of a mated vampire. His eyes flicked to the girl pressed against him, mewling and whimpering in the first throes of Impression. If that *rogue* fucked her, she would be unable to bear off-spring with another.

Worthless.

Alexander made up his mind quickly. "Take the Druids, kill the others."

He did not need Reapers in his coven that did not follow orders. *Or* who took a female breeder he wished to have for himself.

Cole barely had time to lay Rachel down on the cold ground, her breathing shallow, her skin freezing in front of him before the first Reaper was on him.

A Reaper he had been paired with before in battle, against others, who now fought him as an enemy.

Nathan fought by his side, as before. Cole stayed in front of Rachel and the other Druid. Even though it was clear he could not have her.

Duty prevailed. Protect the breeders.

Zach moved Holly behind him protectively. "Stand back, little one," he said to her, caressing her cheek with the pad of his thumb. She wrapped a small hand in the back of his shirt and clung to him. He turned and removed her hand. "I cannot protect you while we are under siege."

"Look out!" Holly screamed and Zach ducked as the swipe of a hand ending in talons narrowly missed where his head had been. He turned and launched himself at the Reaper, his own talons punching out of fingertips that had lengthened to accommodate them.

Holly got low to the ground, crawling to the woman that lay there in the center of the firestorm of fighting. Immediately Holly saw that she was slowly freezing to death and took off her own shoes, putting them on the woman. She took off the parka she wore over another jacket and wrapped the woman's bare legs in it. It was the best she could do and not freeze to death herself.

She covered the woman with her body and watched as the vampire she could hardly breathe without pummeled the other that had come to take her. Holly saw a large vampire advance on her and the woman and she burrowed in deeper beside her, making herself smaller. He looked bad. Worse than the one named Nathan.

Nothing like the one that defended her.

Cole watched Alexander advance on the women and redoubled his efforts to dispatch the Reapers. Nathan and he worked in tandem very well.

It was no different now. Nathan got a strangle hold on with one Reaper, the breath torn from his body and Cole stabbed him in the skull with a talon, twisting it at the last moment, so the brain was scrambled, its signals—gone. The Reaper's body imploded into a pile of ash, as effective as removing the head. He and Nathan turned in time to see Alexander grab the young Druid and she shrieked.

For the *rogue*.

The *rogue* turned from the body of a Reaper he had just decapitated, dumping it like trash at his feet and flung himself toward Alexander. His Druid's blood made him choose rashly, impulsively. For Alexander was a thousand years old and this *rogue* was no match for his stealth.

Cole could see the killing blow blossom from Alexander's hand.

And then Nathan threw himself in the path of it. Committing suicide, saving the *rogue*, giving Cole the chance he needed.

His chest tight, Cole attacked Alexander even as the last of his Reapers fell, a remaining *rogue* standing in triumph over the body, his face a bloody mask in the moonlight.

Cole pierced Alexander from behind, his talons sinking deeply into his back and with a gurgled yell he flung the girl at the ground and Zach scooped her up against him, sprinting away from their fight.

Powerless to stop it, Cole felt Alexander shift to heal his wounds, Cole's hand in the middle of it.

Then he was away, his huge wings taking him into the air and over their heads. Eyes that glowed red looked down on the group for one—two heartbeats. He sailed off, swooping over the tops of the trees, splattered blood on the snow the only sign that Cole had pierced a lung.

Alexander had escaped.

Cole looked for Rachel, took in her strange wardrobe and scooped her up against his chest. Her life was held by the most fragile tether with the blade of the elements against it.

Ready for severing.

8

Cole stood over the frozen ground, the slight hump of the dirt the only marker that his friend, his comrade, Nathan lay beneath the dirt. Not in rest.

In death.

He turned from the hasty grave, the tightness in his chest loosening. His sacrifice would not be in vain. He would take the Druid women and they would flee.

He came into the structure of the *rogue*, a fire blazing in the heart, shutters that kept sunlight out of the interior completely, open for an hour longer. Dawn was approaching. He could feel it pressing at the edges of his consciousness like a warning.

He looked at where Rachel lay, a full grown woman swaddled as if she were a papoose. Still, she would need his blood.

Again.

The third time she had his blood would be the last. Their bond made unbreakable. Only sex, true penetration, would cement it sooner. Right now, to save her extremities he would have to give her blood.

He had also needed to trust the *rogue*. Zach. It went against everything that Cole had been taught in his home coven. But the realization of Alexander's treachery was a fresh and rotting taste in his mouth. Nathan's death motivated him to trust those that before, would have been an impossibility.

He could still smell Zach on her body. He knew they had been together intimately. He seethed. But Cole also knew the hold a mixed blood could have over a Druid. And their final act had not been consummated. It was a breach of trust which struck deep, causing every territorial urge to roar, to scream to take her now, before another could claim her. But as he looked at her fragility by the fire, he was unable to do it.

He would feed her, then they would settle this unrest between them. As it stood now, watching Zach with the new Druid, Holly, curled up in a sleeping ball on his lap, that one would not be after his potential mate. His perfect mate had been handed up to him on a silver platter moments earlier.

They regarded each other across the room. Both unsure of the future of the other.

Could they reconcile their innate differences? Overcome them enough to flee together, begin anew somewhere else? Cole's eyes narrowed on Zach. He did not know.

The *rogue* clutched the small Druid closer, stroking her hair and she made a sound in her sleep, her hand balling into the material of his shirt in a fist, burrowing in closer against him. His eyes darkened in response and he pressed her ever nearer.

I opened my eyes, sweating lightly. My arms were pressed against my sides and when my vision cleared I could see Cole, his intense eyes black in the firelight. Guilt swept over me. I'd let my captor ravage me. I'd responded and all the while Cole had been making his steady way toward me.

Never faltering.

I closed my eyes against the rush of emotion. Tears escaped, leaking out the sides of my eyes.

Then he was there, his arms grasping my shoulders. "Rachel," he said in a low tone of inquiry.

I opened them and what I saw there was acceptance. Not happiness, not yet, but hope.

"I'm sorry. I was confused. I thought I would die… then Erik tried to…" I turned my face away and he brought it back.

"You did nothing wrong. I know how the *rogue* progress. He would have been a fool not to try and mate you. You could not have known what had become of me, where I was." He looked down for a moment and when his eyes locked with mine again, they flashed silver with anger and I shrank back against the fierceness they held.

He unwrapped me from the heavy woolen blanket and when he sat me up, he grasped my shoulders, giving me a small shake. "But you are mine. And soon, we will make it permanent." His eyes searched mine and saw a mirror of his own, uncertainty, hope and fear in a confusing mix.

"I will not force you, but you realize it would be one group or another after you constantly, no matter where you were. You must be mated to cease their pursuit." He rolled up his sleeve and tore into his own wrist.

"Drink," he commanded. I shook my head.

"If you do not, you may lose the use of your hands, feet," he indicated with a sweep of his arm.

I knew that the more blood I had from him, the tighter the pull...bond, whatever the hell he called it, would become. I didn't want to be owned by someone, no matter how they made me feel. I looked at my hands, white even in the firelight and knew he spoke the truth.

I grasped his forearm with both hands, unable to get around the girth of it and pressed my lips to what was offered. It was tangy and sweet, an exquisite assault to my taste buds. Not like the salty taste of copper when I'd bite my lip. I rolled my eyes up to meet his and he moaned his pleasure at my drinking from his vein. The harder I pulled from him, the more I wanted. It frightened me. The neediness.

My greed.

Gently, he extracted me, his hands slightly shaky. "Enough."

He pulled me next to him and with a final look at Zach, and the Druid sleeping against him. He fell asleep with one eye open, staring for a beat at the remaining *rogue*, guarding the door while we slept.

The Vampire, one of the *rogue* and one of the coven of Alexander, shook off the bruises and scars of battle while they slept, their bodies repairing themselves for their next endeavor.

Escape.

EPILOGUE

They ran but remained one step ahead of Alexander.

Throwing themselves across the frozen terrain of Canada they slept were they could, fed on the criminals that were so plentiful, and gathered human food for the women.

Little progress was made in their romances. Their matings. It was primarily about survival.

Cole had a goal. He and Zach had become tight conspirators together. He ruminated on their conversations.

Cole pointed to the map, tapping the route and Zach interrupted him. "No, I believe White Horse Crossing is the very best straightaway." He met Cole's eyes. "The cattle will mask our scent, Reaper." He narrowed his eyes on Cole and he realized that Zach held him partly responsible for Alexander's pursuit.

Zach had a short memory. After all, it was he that had taken Rachel from Cole. His Intimate the one who had perpetuated the worst betrayal. No, if blame was to be meted out, he would share equally.

Zach thought about his next words carefully. "You propose we move toward Seattle, a low-light area." He shrugged. "That latitude, although not ideal, will be enough." Cole nodded. Hopefully, he would see reason. They needed to put their differences aside in the hope of a unified protection of the Druids. Their mates. That is what they would be shortly. When this tireless running stopped.

Cole planted his large hands on his hips, smelling Rachel approach even before she made noise of it.

She came from behind, wrapping her arms around his waist and leaning her head against him. Cole drew her into his body, smelling the hotel shampoo in her hair, thinking it lovely. But it was Rachel. Everything about her moved him. Her fragrance, that which she applied and what was intrinsically *her*. Something he never tired of.

Holly also came to Zach, their relationship different. She was extremely young. Zach may have deliberated the taking of her entirely because of her age, earmarking her acquisition for the future. Nathan had obviously been overcome, beaten and tortured by Alexander, in the insatiable grip of blood lust, he had taken a Druid that was not yet ripe.

Cole had to give grudging admiration to Zach, who as Holly approached, took her tenderly, stroking her jaw, cupping her face like a fragile egg. It was obvious to Cole that the Imprint was true, only their sexual communion needed to finalize it.

Rachel began with her nightly wheedle of him. He understood her need for some human contact but it was dangerous. It was the very thing he wished to avoid.

"Please Cole," she implored. "Just take us to a bar. We'll blend, I swear it."

Zach chuckled. "Yes, our females blend so well." His sarcasm spread thick like jam on toast. Cole gave a grim smile and seeing it, Rachel sighed. He was always so serious. It had been weeks since the threat of Alexander. She crossed her arms across her chest, cradling her breasts.

Cole tried to tear his gaze away from her ripe breasts with an effort. Sleeping together and light kissing was all they'd managed. The four of them needed to find a safe place to land. And it was not here. In this time. It would wait until Seattle.

Holly gave Rachel a grateful look.

"Very well, we will escort you to the human bar. We will eat…"

"We'll eat," Holly giggled and Rachel smiled. The vampires would get their meals outside. In the cold. On the hunt. Rachel knew and shivered. Knowing their victims were the criminal dregs of society didn't make it any easier to justify.

Although, when Cole had relayed the type of blood victims he picked, I couldn't get too worked up about

them. Date rapists? It was a kindness that they didn't cas-
trate them. Jerks.

They got bundled up and the vampires went ahead of
Holly and I, doing a careful reconnaissance before circling
back around to pick us up. It had been three minutes but
I had felt uneasy about Cole's brief absence. How fast I'd
gotten used to him in the role as protector. I felt like a weak
female, a role I wasn't accustomed to. But that was before
creatures of the night began popping up all around me out
of the weird-ass toaster of my new life.

"Where are they?" Holly asked impatiently.

"They'll be here, they're just checking to make sure it's
safe." I liked Holly but sometimes our almost ten year age
gap made an appearance.

Zach didn't seem to mind. They were some kind of
"mated pair." Like some preordained thing. I was trying to
wrap my head around the existence of vampires.

Check.

I'd done that. Then I was trying to further believe that
some strange witch's blood concoction running through
my veins made me a viable breeder for vampires.

Blood suckers, creatures of the night.

Check.

But this? That there were certain Druids that were
perfectly suited...no, only suited to *one* vampire of mixed
descent. It was almost too much.

Like winning a damn lotto ticket or something. I stifled a giggle. It was almost funny.

But then I saw them with my own two eyes and it was the most obvious and natural pairing I'd ever seen. It gave credence to that old saying, "meant to be." Zach hardly let her go to the bathroom without him there.

And now they had not returned. I kept a neutral expression as Holly began to pace.

When it became ten minutes since we'd seen them I went to the hotel door, a room bought from the spoils of the vampires.

Their blood kills.

Cole's voice echoed its warning even as I cracked the door.

Don't ever open it. Don't advertise your scent, your whereabouts.

I wasn't worried.

I opened the door about two inches and met the victorious face of Alexander.

I slammed the door and it burst inward, clipping my injured shoulder. I fell on my back as Holly screamed, running to the bathroom, a vampire behind her in a blur, he ripped her off her feet, covering her mouth.

But it was Alexander that I couldn't take my eyes off. I scuttled backwards from him but he advanced on me.

Hunkering down next to me he whispered, "Where is your precious Reaper now, Druid?"

He lifted a chunk of my hair, smelling it the same way Cole had. But it was so different.

Utterly different.

I wanted to be sick, impotent rage filling me. It beat like a deadly pulse inside my body.

I slapped his smug face.

His expression darkened, my handprint made a livid mark on the paleness of his cold skin.

He backhanded me almost playfully and my head spun. I fell on my back, stunned. My face went numb where he'd struck me.

He hadn't even been trying. Not really.

My eyes met Holly's from the floor, hers wide in a face leveled by fear. The vampire that held her pleased beyond measure. Tears ran down our faces, identical agony.

Alexander jerked me to my feet, pressing me against his side. I swayed and he held me up when all I wanted was to get away from him, my head spinning in streamers of color.

They dragged us to a huge SUV, the exhaust making a lazy spiral like chimney smoke. Holly struggled mightily but the vampire overwhelmed her, she was so tiny. I didn't struggle, my head hurt so bad I was fighting throwing up because of the hit.

Alexander shoved me in first, and got in right after, Holly on the other side with the vampire that held her effectively sandwiching them inside the vehicle. The driver turned, a small smile on his lips. "Where?"

"North," Alexander said, a secret smile on his face.

I hung my head in despair, meeting an identical expression on Holly's face.

Why hadn't Zach and Cole returned for us?

The car pulled away, the town becoming a small, dark dot in the distance as we drove, my hope dimming with my vision.

Cole woke in an alley close to the hotel they were in, his vision filling with Zach, his throat a raw disaster. He crawled over to him, his head swimming.

He did not even want to know what his injuries were. But there was one thing he did know.

Alexander had been the cause of it. The dull ache in his chest told him all he wished to know. There would be frantic tracking ahead of them.

He tore his wrist open like he had done for Rachel by the fire, his teeth clenching at the memory, his fangs puncturing the inside of his own mouth.

He let the blood drip, first onto the wound at Zach's throat, then into a mouth he parted with his strong fingers.

Gradually Cole watched Zach's Adam's apple bob, accepting the lifeblood of their kind and his eyes snapped open, the realization and fear that filled them for one thing and one thing only.

Holly.

His Druid soul mate had been taken from underneath their noses; the ratio of enemies against themselves so high they could not prevail.

While they fought for their lives against ten of their kind, Alexander swept in and took their mates.

Their brides.

Cole looked at the moon, close to setting. He was calculating how much time they would lose when they could finally resume their tracking at night.

A full day.

Cole screamed his rage into the night. Once again Druids were unprotected. Because that was what it was. Rachel would not die. Holly would not die.

But they may very well wish they could.

Before the end, they may wish for death.

Long for it.

HARVEST
Volume Three: The Druid Series
Copyright © 2011-2012 Marata Eros

THE DRUID SERIES 3

HARVEST

MARATA EROS

For my Readers,
without whom, my stories would mean nothing-
Thank you.

1

Zach and Cole worked in tandem, going on pure instinct. The Druids had been taken in a car, while the ground lay frozen all around them in icy stillness.

It was at its most difficult to scent when the temperature was below freezing, as well as the challenge of auto travel tracking.

Unfortunately for Alexander, being a Reaper had its benefits. Cole had extraordinary nasal sensitivity at his disposal. The getaway car, as it were, was unique to his kiss' compound. Therefore, it had a signature that he could trace.

That he did trace.

Then there was Zach. Zach had fallen into a true mated pairing with Holly. One in which he was bonded to her by blood. They had shared blood more than the mandatory three cycles. It had given Zach, of the shared Druid ancestry, daylight privileges.

Cole had also taken from Rachel. As a pureblood she gave him that benefit as well. He could only pray to whatever was holy, that Alexander had not thought to pierce the veins that lay beneath his grasp. Essentially, a blood rape.

His large hands clenched into meaty hammers of violence with just the thought of their predatory former leader harming Rachel. Taking what was not his to have.

Cole's thoughts turned to Holly. She was obviously related. He and Zach and he had conferred and they were of matching blood. Rachel and Holly were siblings, there was no doubt.

Who were the relatives that had given the girls up? Had it been done purposefully? As a measure of protection? Or, was there something other afoot?

Many questions without answers.

Cole thought through all these things, running seamlessly in his mind as he and Zach ran the frozen terrain together, sleeping little during the day, waking to feed during the night. Their pursuit of Alexander and the gap therein, closing with each minute that passed.

They drew close, Rachel's unique biological perfume proliferating everywhere he scented. Maybe they had bedded down somewhere that had another vampire contingent? That possibility snaked its way down a spine that was stiff with apprehension.

They moved as one toward a local bar, nearly to the Alaska/Canadian border, backtracking.

"Are we near?" Zach asked, eyes drowning pools of black ink. The light all around them bright, undimmed by the night, the moon full and luminously brilliant above them.

Cole nodded, not speaking. They were here to feed. They needed to be fully vested with blood if they were to engage Alexander and whatever contingent he had garnered on the three day journey since the women had been taken.

Zach and he moved to the back alley, where there were always the human dregs, scurrying about in the dark.

Like the rodents they were.

My tears had dried, my sobbing gone unheeded. The cloth pressed between my lips and that bound its way around my skull was pulled tight.

I rolled my eyes to where Holly was, hers wide with fright.

The women hung, suspended. Their toes barely grazed the concrete floor, shoulders numb.

Alexander smiled. Everything he had dreamed of possessing was here before him. He would have them both, he had decided. Who was to tell him differently? When he tired of them, and his blood lust was well sated, he would turn them over to whatever Reaper had sufficient ancestry to breed them out.

It was a perfect plan. Fool proof.

His eyes roamed the form of Rachel, ripe and curved, her blood a fragrant wine ready to be consumed. He moved forward, the muffled sounds of the other Druid, muted by the binding stuffed in her mouth.

I watched Alexander come closer, violence in motion and despaired, he would have me. Bleed me.

And judging by the way he looked, the other as well.

It was all because of my moment of curiosity at the door. I should've never opened it. It put myself and Holly at risk. Right now, I felt like a goddamned loser. I'd let Holly get taken. It was my fault. Whatever he did, I was determined to survive it.

For Cole.

I felt my guts clench at the first stroke of a finger along my jaw. I couldn't help the involuntary flinch for anything in the world.

Josiah looked at their supposed leader and felt disquiet enter him. Alexander had once been a great leader, meting out Druid fairly amongst the Druid vampire, Reapers especially.

How had the circumstances lent themselves to the debauchery at hand? He was unsure. But he could not abide two pure Druids, the kiss having gone so long without one of pure descent, to be treated in this despicable manner. And why would Alexander be tormenting the women as he was? He gave a hard gaze to the other Reapers, the few that had survived the massacre at the *rogue's* stronghold and they nodded back.

They were of one mind.

The three moved forward to overwhelm their leader. Their leader who appeared to have gone mad.

Alexander felt the Reapers at his back before they were upon him.

I widened my eyes in the only warning I could give as the closest Reaper approached Alexander. A tremulous hope blossomed within my soul that there may yet be freedom as the first talon buried itself within Alexander's back.

Alexander felt the pierce of talon to flesh as he twisted around to meet the assault with one of his own. He buried his fingers, turned to sharpened claws, into the underside of the jaw of the one who attacked first. Another Reaper used the fighting as a distraction to take Alexander's head.

With a sweeping blow, he struck Alexander from behind, relieving him of his thought process forever. His head rolled away like a bowling ball on the concrete floor in a spray of blood and gore, the mess spreading as it flew.

The Reapers looked down at Josiah as he gasped for breath, his eyes trained on Andrew's face. He made a decision. Using a claw like a knife, he released the bound Druid who was closest. She fell into the arms of his brethren and he gave her a look. His eyes slid to the pile of ash which used to be Alexander. Their leader's custom made clothes lay atop his remains.

Andrew gave a grim smile and said to the Druid, "You will need to give this Reaper blood. Now."

I sagged into the arms of the Reaper that held me in abject relief, watching the one that had decapitated Alexander. I was so grateful I could spit but of course there would be payment. I knew this.

I narrowed my eyes at his request.

Cole had told me that every drink of my pure Druid blood brought the vampire closer to walking in the light.

The sun would no longer be their enemy.

Fear seized my guts. It would not be just one sip. They'd bleed me dry.

I knew it.

I struggled uselessly, weakened by everything we'd been through, my arms swinging like loose noodles at my sides.

Andrew dragged her to Josiah, his neck a ruined disaster, his gasping breaths that rattled made her back up even as she was pulled forward.

Andrew placed her wrist at his mouth.

Josiah sucked in a huge breath and clamped down on the proffered wrist.

I couldn't help it, that much pain as the fangs sunk into my wrist was more than I could bear.

I wailed as they struck.

The one named Andrew was beside me instantly as I whimpered in pain. "We do not wish to hurt you purposefully. *He dies*. He will die without what you possess. If there were any other way, we would not force this."

I nodded. What could I do? While he sucked at my wrist, mewling like a cat with cream as he lapped my blood, I closed my eyes. Shame, terror and something else warred together in a confusing wash of emotions. All this accomplished was buying myself some time.

When I could think past the pain, my eyes met Holly's. Her's were wide with terror, mine with resolve.

2

Cole and Zach circled the group that they had discovered.

Vampire.

They had been careless, running across their own kind, the wind blowing the wrong direction to alert them until they were upon them.

The male Cole took for the leader hissed at Cole, warning him off his prey.

As if Cole would consider it, he could smell the drug-addled blood from here. He was welcome to it.

"You are not of this region. You smell foreign. By what rights do you hunt here?" the leader asked, the blood from his victim making his mouth resemble that of a clown.

Zach and Cole gave each other a full glance. They were sorely outnumbered, five to two. He would play the civility hand and see where it got him.

"We are but passing through. Actually, we are in search of Druid."

The leader's brows quirked. "You are Reapers?" His eyes slid to Zach.

"I am not. I am *rogue*," Zach said.

They regarded one another for a moment then the leader said, "Yet...you hunt together. A Reaper and one of the *rogue*. In search of Druid flesh." He chortled out loud. "That is the first I have ever heard of such a thing."

Cole knew that he sought information but would not aide them. He moved to leave.

The leader of the four other vampires gave a subtle signal to his comrades in arms.

They surrounded Zach and Cole.

They moved closer to each other, back to back.

Josiah looked up with rapture as the Druid offered her life-saving blood to him. Albeit reluctantly. But who could blame the Druid women their wariness? Alexander had been cruel to this breeder, true. And the other, who he had not given so much as a glance to, would have been treated similarly. Why he had become a tyrant when he had once ruled with fairness, he did not know. When Josiah felt that he could breathe again, his ruined esophagus mending itself as he drank, he released the Druid's wrist.

But not before he lapped at the wound, the ragged edges an embarrassment. His usual finesse had been absent in the face of the scent of her blood and his death a near thing.

The Reaper finally released my wrist after licking it for what seemed like forever. The saliva he'd used like a salve. It wasn't a burning mess anymore. I cradled my ragged wrist against my chest and gave accusing eyes to Andrew.

He shrugged his shoulders. "It was no small thing to kill Alexander. Our leader. Our leader for millennia." His eyes never left mine.

I gulped and backed away.

Into Josiah. The one I'd just given blood to.

Wow, that was speedy.

I whirled around to defend myself against the impossible and he was smiling, revealing fangs. "I would no more hurt you than I would myself, breeder. We will not give you the end for which Alexander had planned."

I didn't ask what that end would have been.

"But neither do we feel inclined to return you to our comrade, Cole." Andrew elaborated.

I opened my mouth to protest but Holly threw herself in my arms just as I would have given old Andrew a piece of my mind. Where my bravery came from, I didn't know. But I sure as hell was tired of being passed around, pursued and now...caught.

I was on the bad side of pissed off at the vamp at my back. The one that met my eyes got it.

Holly pressed against me in near-hysteria and I stroked her hair as she cried.

"Cole has shared some of your history with me," I said to Andrew and he crossed his arms, the ash of his leader as backdrop. I shivered, going on, "The *rogue* he travels with is a true mate to Holly." My eyes shifted to the tiny girl I was holding. So miniature I felt like she was a doll in the circle of my arms.

"Nathan died to protect her, so she could be with Zach. It would seem to me that you vamps need to rein in your instinct to breed us long enough to think about what kind of parents we'd be to your offspring," I paused, letting that soak in then continued, "*if* we're forced into relationships that go against your own rules."

That had been quite a speech for me but I saw the wheels turning in Andrew's head as he began to pace back and forth in front of me. *In profile, with his hair bound by a leather tie, he looked every bit the arrogant European*, I thought randomly.

"Are you certain?" he asked me, turning those hawkish features to me.

I shrugged. "That's what Cole said."

"What does the girl say? Does she acknowledge the tie?"

Holly pulled away, her face a tear stained mess and with a trembling lip, slowly nodded.

"This little slip of a girl?" he asked in a derisive tone, flipping his palm toward her dismissively. "How old are you girl?"

I could see what it took for Holly not to cower, her only sign that the crying jag was still within reach was a pouty lower lip that she clenched softly between her teeth. But when she spoke, her voice was clear, sniffles gone.

"I don't know what all this 'mating' stuff means. But what I felt for him, even knowing he's one of you guys... a vampire," she looked at Andrew, and Josiah, who had made his way to stand beside the other vampire, "told me it's real." She put her fist against her heart, her words only a little shaky.

Josiah and Andrew looked at each other and Andrew said, "You will eventually come to care for one of us. We cannot just allow you to be with a *rogue*. As it were, we cannot even be sure why a true mating would come about with one of them." He shrugged.

I narrowed my eyes on them. "So what you've just told us, if I'm understanding your jerkness here, is that you'll be mating with us anyway. It doesn't matter that even as we speak, there may be two very pissed off vampires on your ass."

Andrew smiled, then it faded as he thought of Cole. That one bore concern. The *rogue* was without concern. Except...if the mating was a true fact, that the *rogue* was indeed the true mate of the young Druid.

He would stop at nothing to regain her.

Nothing.

Andrew frowned. "Let us leave this place. We will take of your blood and you will submit. This will allow daylight travel."

He, Josiah and the three others walked toward us.

Holly did cower then.

I was resolute. They could take all they want. At the first opportunity, I would escape.

After all, they killed Alexander to free us from his plans, only to put their designs on us without our consent.

More of the same, I was thinking.

Their huge bodies drew closer as my heart sped at their proximity.

Cole and Zach unsheathed their talons, the claws bursting their houses of flesh instantly, a punching sounded as their fingertips released their charge.

The leader circled, his talons at the ready. "We do not have to war with you and the *rogue*. Tell us where the Druids are and we will give chase. Our numbers are greater, concede our advantage. We will not harm the breeders." He smiled and continued, "But we *will* breed them," he said definitively, spreading his palms away from his body.

Cole would not stop his pursuit of Rachel until the breath left his body. He did not need to confer with Zach, a true mate to a Druid was formidable. Cole was not yet mated to Rachel and now lamented his decision to wait until they were settled. He was sure that Zach echoed his thoughts.

"I see that your decision has been made," the leader said in a low voice, attacking as the last word was uttered.

Zach was *rogue* and did not know the meaning of fair fighting. He slung his bladed hands low, taking the testicles of the advancing vampire right at the root. With a shrieking wail, he fell where he stood, blood spraying out between fingers that held his nethermost regions in a stranglehold. Zach had crippled him, stunning his advance in its tracks.

Let him grow a pair, Zach thought without humor, his thoughts already trained on Holly. He would do whatever needed to be done to get to her.

No tactic was beneath his notice.

Cole would have laughed at Zach's cunning if he was not instantly engaged with the leader and who looked to be his first. Cole smashed his talons in the face of his first even as his downward stroke cut deeply into Cole's shoulder where he had just laid the strike. His arm was useless, falling numb under the assault and he took the enemy down with a skull scramble. Cole used his shitkicker to roundhouse kick the leader as he let his body fall backward to avoid a well-placed swipe at where his head had been moments before.

Two others came from behind as Cole was falling. They tried to catch him but Cole was accustomed to practiced falls of avoidance and as his toe made purchase with the leader's jaw, crushing it on impact like so much glass, he used his good hand to balance his fall and both of his legs came above his head and twined around the head of one of the other's.

Cole twisted his legs, his palm flat on the abandoned alley pavement, the cold leeching into his arm and shoulder as the strain of holding up two hundred and thirty pounds of tense muscle was executed on a dime of motion.

He broke the neck of the one as the leader fell to the floor, unable to scream from a mouth that could not longer form words.

The *rogue* came for the last. The enemy saw his problem and the vampire came at Zach, odds as they were, and with practiced jabs was overtaking him. But Zach had one more thing up his sleeve, allowing his upper shoulder to be hooked by talons that went through his body and perforated his back with a grunt, he head-butted the vampire, stunning him. Zach smashed the Reaper's skull with the nubs of his partially extended talons.

Like brass knuckles.

The brains of the vampire slid out his ears, the Reaper's talons retracting automatically upon his death and slicing through the meat of Zach's shoulder with an agonizing jerk.

Cole lay on the ground. His shoulder was a numb disaster, his bell certainly rung and looked at Zach as he advanced on the injured enemy ranks.

Seconds later, the Reapers were dead, three heads leveled against the frozen road. Zach held out a hand to Cole.

He took it.

They turned together, the soles of their boots becoming dirty with snow and ash.

Scenting the air for prey, they did not have far to go.

They fell on the group of drug addicts. Weak from fighting, the finickiness of before gone, the need for food forgotten in the face of their need.

Zach and Cole drank.

Adding the bodies of their prey to the ashen snow which lay like storm clouds on the ground.

3

I was laying in a languid stupor. One of Alexander's wonderful Reaper spawn cradled me against his chest, too weak to move. They'd had their pound of flesh.

Or in this case, a pound of blood.

They'd had just enough so that I was still conscious. Holly continued whimpering beside me.

Apparently, when you were a true mate, having another vampire take blood was extra painful.

Swell.

The males had felt bad about taking from her. But not bad enough to stop.

The Reapers surrounded an old warehouse, the wind and snow howling around where they stood. I had my eyelids at half-mast, every fiber of energy going to keeping myself awake when Andrew spoke. "Josiah, Elias...get the women in there for the night to bed down. They are too weak by far to withstand the storm. My brothers..." The group looked at Andrew expectantly and what he said next

195

made me want to punch him square in the face, "because of the richness of our meal, we will be able to travel with the sun one day hence."

There were muted cheers but the wind sucked away the sound of them.

Good for them, I thought sourly.

They kicked in the door that stood between them and the heated building, its large windows intersected with many panes of glass, jewel-like in the moonlight which pierced their dirty surfaces.

They gathered tough woolen military blankets that smelled like they must have been from WWII at least. They lowered me into a cocoon of them and wrapped me up like a fragile parcel.

"Will she be well enough to travel tomorrow?" The one named Josiah asked Andrew.

He looked at me critically before responding, "I think that if she rests, then consumes some food, she will be well enough."

I glanced down at my forearms, punctured as they were with the pockmarks of multiple fang piercings and wanted to cry. I looked like Swiss cheese.

Instead of crying, I let exhaustion take me and fell into an uneasy recuperative slumber.

Little did I know that as I slept, Cole came for me, scenting the blood droplets that had fallen as the others feasted on my blood.

His howl of rage never reached my deaf ears as I slept from exhaustion and blood loss, my forearms a throbbing burning rawness.

Cole's mouth snapped shut, the echoing of his bellow of rage still flinging its music around the space where they had discovered the trail.

Cole and Zach had found the blood trail which told them that Rachel and Holly were now in the hands of his fellow Reapers.

It also heralded the demise of Alexander.

A superb development.

But what enraged Cole was the scent of Holly and Rachel's blood everywhere.

Then there was the scarf that Holly always wore. Zach had it clutched in his big hands, pressing it against his face like a cat rubbing its scent along a favorite couch. His eyes were clenched tightly. "They took her blood at the neck," his voice was low gravel tinged with despair.

A grave insult to violate the intimacy of a mated vampire spouse.

But they were not truly mated. Sexual intercourse was needed before that would truly happen with finality, bonded forever.

"Why did I not take her before they did?"

He was not talking kidnapping, Cole knew. He was talking about burying his cock and seed in the chosen Druid.

Cole shrugged, understanding exactly their complacency. They never thought it possible that Alexander could best them. If they could have just made it to Seattle. Then they would've disappeared within the folds of its concrete embrace and they would have been as invisible as needed.

Now, because of their disregard for the potential of the Druid women's capture, they were gone, like so much sand falling through fingers.

Cole picked up the silken shirt that had been Alexander's, the cufflinks falling to the ground at his feet, twinkling in the moonlight. He scooped them up, pocketing their weight.

Easy pawning.

Zach tucked the scarf in his pocket, so slight it hardly showed.

They nodded at each other and easily picked up the trail. With the slimmest hope, Cole believed it was possible that the Reapers did not know who followed them.

But knowing Rachel as he did, she might have used the threat of them as a way to prevent or postpone just what had occurred.

No matter, they fed on the women to run during the day. If they had traveled in a quad, then there were four Reapers.

Cole smiled grimly. They had just done away with worse odds. As they ran, Cole spoke to Zach in the high speech of their kind, heard only by a lone dog in the distance.

It howled at the unnaturalness of their speech, tucking its tail between its legs and burrowing into the safety of its den. One eye was kept on the dark terrain outside his kennel. The dog was hopeful that the dead creatures would not turn in his direction.

He slunk further inside his doghouse.

I awoke naked and spreadeagled on the blankets I'd fallen
asleep on.

A vampire loomed a each of the four corners of my
body. I sucked in a lungful and was about to scream when
a hand covered my mouth. I looked up into the eyes of the
one that had first taken my blood and realized that they
wanted more than the pound of blood they'd consumed.

I was thinking the pound of flesh hadn't been far off.

Muddled thoughts of Cole stirred in my mind, but
Andrew was between my legs and the heat that mingled
with their blood's call to mine wasn't something I could
rationalize away. He saw that I had awoken and braced a
forearm against my hips even as my panties had been torn
off my body.

"Spread your legs, breeder," Andrew growled.

I had enough resistance to attempt to close them even
as he used large hands to push them apart. I gulped back
a scream as Josiah captured the sound with his kiss. His

tongue invaded my mouth, stabbing in and out the warm entrance, fucking it as I moaned against the invasion.

Andrew mirrored the dance of his tongue with his fingers, pushing one deep in my pussy, pulling it out, adding a second and generating a rhythm as if tailor-made for me. My breaths were coming in ragged gasps as he was bringing me closer.

I internally damned my biology. A biology that put me at risk to fuck any Reaper or breedable vampire that walked by.

One of the other vampires had my arms cranked above my head as my body was pushed and pulled subtly with the pumping of Andrew's fingers. Just as I thought I would blast an orgasm around his fingers he removed them and one of his foot soldiers took over. Instead of burying his fingers in my snatch, he put his tongue in me, sweeping it along my heated folds and alternately stabbing the warm, thick length of it inside my hot hole.

I couldn't help it, I spread my legs wider to give a vampire I'd never met before today greater access. He took it for the invitation is was and tore his pants open. His great cock sprung free of the trappings of his pants and seeing it like a great sword of flesh made me shiver in anticipation.

He lowered himself on me, hovering above my wet entrance even as my hips strained to meet his. He began to inch the blunt tip of his staff inside my wet pussy. He groaned with pleasure as the beginning of him entered me and I thrust my hips upward to meet each inch he slowly shoved into me.His girth was large and my pussy had to stretch to accommodate him. But the pull of his cock as it sunk in and out was delicious. As he reached the end of my channel, I felt the bump of him at its end and I cried out as the pleasure nearly overwhelmed me.

Josiah came beside him and said, "How does the breeder feel wrapped around you?" he asked in a voice gone low with desire and barely masked lust.

The vampire above me grunted as he pounded his length inside me and ground out, "She fucks true, my friend. As you'll see soon enough."

The vampires had let my arms go, satisfied to stand around me in a loose circle, while their comrade buried the flesh of his cock to the root inside me, my body sliding back and forth by the pounding.

I watched his shoulders bunch and flex as he buried himself in me and I spread my legs wider so he could get deeper penetration. He stabbed his length deep inside me one last time and shuddered his release. Hot seed filled my body, soaking my pussy, which throbbed its pleasure around his thick shaft, milking it of every last drop.

He pulled out, and Josiah took his place. Guiding his flesh inside mine, cum leaking out from its predecessor, he slid inside me in one long push. Both of us grunted with the impact, my pussy wet and ready to receive his cock.

He clenched his teeth, a flutter appearing in his jaw as he rocked inside me. "I will not last long, breeding you will be a pleasure," he said as he lowered his lips on mine, giving me a feather's kiss that tweaked my mouth open. He braced one hand behind my head, holding his weight above me as he plunged inside me, the other hand buried in my hair, training my head in the direction he wanted it to be. His lips moved over mine with force now, even as his body entered mine. As he drew closer, he licked a long line against my bottom lip as he pumped his last into me. His hands left my hair to slap the floor beneath me. Josiah arched his back, our hips met, married deeply within each other's flesh.

Andrew hauled Josiah off roughly, his shaft, now soft from use and release, torn out like a fleshy plug.

"I have waited a long time to bury my flesh in a breeder."

I came to my senses and squirmed onto all fours, trying to scramble away. His total attitude screamed ownership, devour, plunder and I *was* intimidated. I'd never screwed two men in a row and wasn't wanting to make it three. Especially not with him.

He grasped my hips from behind and jerking me against him, plunged a cock so huge into me that I gasped, the pleasure bordering pain.

"Oh yes…she feels…perfect," he grunted as he forced himself into my dripping pussy.

Wet with the cum of others.

The more I tried to get away the harder he held my hips, pushing his engorged cock deep inside of me.

"Hold still breeder, just a few more strokes of my prick inside your ready pussy and I will sink my fangs into you."

I really tried to move then and he plunged harder, my pussy making a sucking sound around his cock. The tight, wet hole, clinging to his prick as it rode me.

"Now, you will be mine!" he shouted as his release shot up into my womb, the entrance sucking up all the seed he spurted out of his cock as he sank his fangs into the soft flesh of my neck. His body arched above mine, his dick still pumping, my hips rising against my will, spreading and thrusting against him.

His throat convulsed as he took my blood even as he sprayed his cum into my snatch.

Andrew pulled out of me and pushed my head to the floor, my ass and pussy primed in the air, cum leaking down my inner thighs. He slapped my ass with a stinging softness that made me moan. I hadn't wanted to take pleasure in the fucking but it felt so natural for the Reapers to fuck me.

Even as the next one moved into position behind my cunt I spread my legs wider. He found my entrance quickly and slammed his dick all the way inside me. This one spared me nothing, finding my hole wet with others' seed, he plowed into my pussy, pumping ferociously. Using his vampire speed he slid in and out, rubbing deliciously over that spot up high that would give me what I needed.

"Is she coming?" I heard one of the Reapers ask.

"Not...yet!" the one that I couldn't see threw out through teeth that were clamped together. He was working his control to get as much fucking of my wet pussy as he could before his release.

His dick moved inside me in a blur and as his shaft hardened, my womb opened and my throbbing pussy clenched around his cock, inviting his release in an undeniable need.

"Oh God!" he yelled and poured all the cum he'd been holding back inside me. He shoved my head down with a massive hand on my neck and held me still as he continued to pump his cock inside me.

I moaned in pleasure as that fourth cock left my throbbing hole.

I flipped over on my back and waited for any others, my pussy a burning mass of heat and desire.

I felt like a bitch in heat as I lay there, legs spread, my glistening and well-used hole open for more.

<hr />

"Rachel, Rachel! Wake up!"

I opened my eyes and gazed into Holly's worried eyes.

My pussy was still throbbing.

From the dream.

That whole thing had been an erotic nightmare.

It had been tasteable; it felt so real.

I threw a forearm over my eyes, confused and relieved at the same time. It had seemed so real. I opened my eyes again and looked at the healing evidence of fangs and wondered about side effects.

Maybe they took my blood and then…I didn't know.

Holly searched my eyes. "You were moaning in your sleep. They wanted me to check on you first, so you wouldn't freak out."

Right, *not* freaking out here. Just had the biggest orgasm of my life in my sleep but wasn't touched.

I sat up, looking at my surroundings in the daylight. Blinking several times my eyes met those of Andrew's and he smirked.

He totally knew.

I got to my feet, feeling lightheaded from the blood that was taken and the residual effects of coming eighty times. I stalked over to Andrew and I said, "What did you do to me?" I stabbed my finger into his muscular chest to emphasize my words and he captured it, bringing it to his mouth, kissing it softly. "Nothing you did not wish done, breeder."

"Bullshit!" I jerked my hand away and he laughed. "What...you come in and rape me in my dreams? Is that what this is about?"

His face became carefully neutral. "It is only one benefit of the blood share. We have taken of your blood. For a few days now, we may walk in the day, glory in the heat of the sun upon our skin. And, we have access to your mind while you are not conscious." His eyes held mine. "You begrudge us the encounter that we had with you?"

No. "Hell yes!" I said. It didn't really matter that I'd ended up having some of the hottest sex of my life. If it had not been for being Druid, would I have allowed it? My thoughts turned to Michelle, my friend that had been a lover of casual sex. Was I like that now? I didn't think I had come around to that mindset so quickly. But this biology. The biology of being Druid, was a sexual magnet to the Reapers.

Then there was Cole.

I was sure he was the one I was destined to be with. Once mated, I wouldn't be sexual fodder for the masses. I straightened my spine. "That was exploiting me. You want to use us as breeders for your offspring? You said you 'saved us' from Alexander?" My voice dropped to a whisper, being vampire, he didn't even strain to hear. "You just traded one bad behavior for another." My eyes searched the burgundy irises of his. "Fine. You've proven that I can't resist the pull of our blood."

Andrew's brows rose in surprise.

I continued, "But all you did was play your hand, force it. Have some damn self-pride and conquer us the right way. Don't use..."

"Trickery?" Josiah said with a grin.

I nodded. "Yeah, that'll do."

Holly walked up beside me, looking like she had measles on her arms too.

"Duly noted," Andrew said. "We will not...indispose you in the future." His voice became intense, "but know this, we will have you, all of us, and you will welcome it."

I didn't say anything but I think my face conveyed what my silence did not: fat chance.

5

Cole watched with anger as the bloody orb of the sun sunk beneath the horizon, low already because of the season.

He knew not where Rachel was, but was convinced that the ones who had her had consumed her blood. They were daywalkers now. Not for long, no. But, they had lead time that he and Zach did not enjoy. Cole swore softly, beating his fist into his open palm.

Zach swung his face to Cole's. "They have partaken of Holly's blood," he said, seething. His face was a mask of rage and Cole clapped him on his back.

"They are Reapers, Zach. With Alexander gone, they will hold to the regime."

Zach looked at Cole. "That is what worries me. The *rogue* hold to one mate for one vampire. Your kiss practices multi-partner matings."

Cole sighed. "It has been the way of it for many years. However," he pegged Zach with his intense stare, "in this case, there can only be two mates to the exclusion of all others. She will consummate with two. The key is to reach the Druids before they have executed this."

"Do they not wish to abide by the ritual?"

Cole's face took on a grim look. "That is the way. But, in the presence of pure Druids, for the length of journey back to our coven…" Cole spread his hands wide. "They would have to master a level of self-restraint that may be impossible. Think back on the challenge of it with the women when they were with us. Even with all the running, we still wanted them."

Zach thought about tiny Holly. A body made to fuck his. His hands shook with the need to bury himself inside her. In all her virginal splendor. Untried, but for him. *Soon*, he promised himself. Somehow he held out hope that the Reapers would leave her as she be, that only her blood would be consumed to bind and aide them in their travel back to their home coven.

But there was no guarantee.

They readied themselves for pursuit.

Yet again.

Holly and I clung together as we entered a boisterously loud and filthy tavern with one of the Reapers. The patrons yelled at each other, swinging full and frosted mugs of ale around to punctuate the points of their conversation. Holly looked shell-shocked but I knew she hadn't been subjected to the Reapers brand of illicit entertainment while she dozed. Oh-no. They intuited that she might be damaged from such treatment.

Or so I hoped.

I was not so sure that I hadn't been. I shook it off, looking for a server in the dim corners of the establishment. No one.

I was literally starving to death, remembering my conversation with Josiah.

"You will eat, if we have to force feed you. You have given blood and will now need to replenish it with human sustenance."

No shit, I thought uncharitably.

So here I was, with Holly the nineteen-year old who needed babysitting, tagging along. I was grumping because of the gnawing in my body and the uneasy sexual union that had been breached. And of course, my personal favorite, the future of being their prize breeding stock.

No pressure.

The Reaper, whose name was Elias, indicated for us to sit down in the booth. I slid in and turned immediately to look out the grimy window, all four corners shadowed with the nicotine of years of smoking but allowed no longer. Only the filth remained to tell the history.

I looked away from the blackness of the night revealed outside. I was so tired my body ached and Holly's head lay against my shoulder, her hand in mine.

A waitress approached the table, chewing the cud of her gum like a cow. The corner of Elias' mouth turned up. I could almost hear what he was thinking. The Reapers were such an amusing group. Not.

He greeted her and turned to us. "The women are quite hungry. What do you recommend off your extensive menu?"

I almost laughed. Those Reapers, they sounded so natural. I did a mental eye-roll.

The "extensive menu" was a greasy fingerprint-coated paper with five items. Loved the sense of humor on these guys.

"I'll have a burger and fries," I said quietly, keeping my amusement out of ordering.

Elias looked at Holly. "Make that two," she said, the fear barely contained. She hadn't warmed up to the Reapers. After my story of the dream sharing, she wasn't feelin' it.

I heard that.

The waitress turned to me with eyes that were glassy. "Ya want cheese with that, miss?"

"Yes, thank you."

Elias looked at me for a long moment. "It is not what you think, you know."

I thought it was everything I was speculating and more but didn't respond.

Taking my silence as encouragement he continued, "We will not force you. You will choose two Reapers." His eyes slid to Holly and his glance encompassed her as well.

She shivered beside me.

Our food came and we ate like robots. I shoveled about half the meal before becoming too stuffed. A lot of that was probably just lack of eating. I bet my stomach was the size of a walnut.

I looked at Holly, who I was sure was about one hundred pounds. She shook her head, pushing her half finished food into the center of the table.

Elias cocked his brow. "It is not good? I was told this was the best greasy spoon in the area."

I barked out a laugh. What he said sounded so contrived. I didn't think the vampires got out much. Holly turned and smiled at me. She got it.

He looked confused and I relieved him of that, "You guys need to work on blending in. Ya know, verbally. Nobody on the damn planet says 'greasy spoon' anymore." He scowled at me and I smiled back sweetly. I did a mental tally on my side. Whatever gave me a little advantage with the group pleased the hell outta me.

He threw cash on the table in a semi-huff and we walked outside.

I wouldn't have been so cavalier had I know what was going to greet me when we returned to the place that the Reapers had broken into.

Holly and I watched in shocked horror as four Reapers screwed human women, in various stages of fangs latched onto veins.

Holly had to turn away into my shoulder and I hissed at Elias, "Oh yeah, this is really warming us up to your cause."

He returned fire in a low voice, "We have needs, Druid. Unless you wish to provide those needs, both sexual and in blood payment, I suggest you let us have our way with them. Besides," he looked at the carnal orgy in front of him, "they enjoy our attentions immeasurably."

Rachel watched as the four Reapers rutted above women, spread and moaning. One shrieked as she came while a Reaper bit her, her rapture at the intensity of her orgasm as he drilled her from above was obvious to even the least astute observer.

"They're raping them," Holly moaned. Elias turned to her, lifting her chin with a finger. "No, little one, they are being pleasured by vampire. They will give their lifeblood to us so that we may live another day."

Holly jerked her face away from Elias and he turned away from her, shrugged out of his jacket. He moved with an almost predatory glide toward a woman who lay on the floor under thrall, her eyes locking on his as he moved toward her.

"Spread your legs, human."

I watched as she did it, her heels almost horizontal to her body. He tore off her panties and said as a command, "You are aroused, wet for the taking. You cannot wait to have my cock inside you."

The woman writhed on the floor, her hips rising slightly, her pussy folds glistening with moisture and open to receive his cock. Elias opened the fly on his black leather pants and a cock as thick as my wrist filled his hand.

He slid it into the woman, her hips pushing aggressively against his entry. She shouted at the violent thrust. I watched as his ass muscles clenched and loosened as he plowed every bit of his meat into her waiting hole. None too gentle, he was giving her his entire length and she was taking it, her legs shaking...then she came, trembling all around him and he sped to vampire speed, his tight ass a blur as he plunged into her waiting cunt.

I looked around at the others, noticing some of the vamps had moved on to the women's asses. The pussies so completely used, they'd taken a new hole for their pleasure. Putting fingers into the pussies full of cum, scooping some out, they put fingers into the tight asses of the women. All of them with their hips high and their faces planted on the floor. Begging to be fucked in the ass.

The orgy unfolded all around me. The vampires worked in unison, plugging the waiting asses of the women, they had used their cum like lubricant and were pumping away on the women's tight rose buds. As I watched, one Reaper gave a light swat to one of the women, his prick buried in her bud to the root and she moaned, shoving her hips backward against him for a deeper lock on his flesh.

He grabbed her hair and jerked her head back, looking at me while he did her, bucking into her so hard her breasts smacked against each other making a fleshy sound of their own.

I met Andrew's eyes and knew he was thinking of the dream where he'd ridden my pussy as he was riding this human woman's ass.

I turned on my heel and took Holly with me, we escaped to another room.

Anywhere not to see the vampires latched like snakes on women that would be whores for them under their compulsion.

I was disgusted by them.

I was also aroused. Having had a taste of what a vampire could make my body feel as he buried his tool of flesh inside of me. I clenched my eyes, keeping my thoughts trained on Cole.

Please come quickly, I pleaded silently. Before I become a slut for the Reapers.

Holly whispered in my ear, "They're going to do that to us soon."

I shook my head. "Only if we say yes. They can't use thrall on us."

Holly's lip trembled. "I'm scared, but it's exciting too."

I looked at her. "What do you mean? You told me you'd never had sex."

She looked at me, embarrassed. "I haven't," she rolled her lip into her teeth, biting it softly. "But, it makes me hot here," she said pointing to her pussy.

I guess the Druid biology was already working. Priming her for use. Untried or not. She may not have that title for long.

I shuddered to think about a virgin in the hands of Reapers. All four.

Elias walked in just then, he looked at Holly, sniffing the air. He gave her a smile.

"You smell of heat and sex, Druid."

Holly cowered against me and I said, "Don't you touch her. You just had a human, you don't need her."

His eyes were hooded and he looked at Holly. "Do you want my fingers and tongue inside you, little Druid."

Holly stood and began to take off her pants.

"No!" I yelled. "Holly no!"

She didn't listen, tears streaming down her face. "I'm sorry, I just have to have some relief. Zach took me to the brink, always saying he'd finish it when we got somewhere safe. I want to be a virgin but I have to...I need..."

"I know what you need, little Druid," he said softly. And before she could react he was on her, tearing her panties down to her ankles and I stood there and watched helplessly as he buried his face in her pussy, lapping at her cunt while she whimpered and begged for more, helpless before the biological directive that we shared.

Holly felt so guilty. She was the perfect mate of Zach, but he had made her sexually frustrated. She spread her legs as the vampire put his tongue on the nub of her clit and sucked it until she cried out. Holly knew that he might fuck her but she couldn't stop herself. Her pussy felt so ripe. As he suckled her clit she shoved her pussy in his face and he chuckled. "So eager," he murmured. He began to put a finger in her hole. "Oh…so tight. You feel so tight. Please…little Druid, let me put my shaft in you until I reach your barrier."

Holly knew she should say no but it would technically keep her a virgin, her barrier still in place.

She let her legs fall open to receive what he offered and Rachel said, "Don't Holly."

Holly didn't listen, her pussy dripping with honey.

Elias couldn't wait to penetrate this Druid. He would not really be taking her virginity but he would explore the tightness of her flesh as far as he could.

He did, pushing his shaft into her wet folds, the tightness of her almost unbearable, like a velvet stranglehold she caressed him. He wanted to shove his length inside her the whole way, pinning her beneath him but he held back. He began a slow pump and knew he wouldn't last. She was so fucking tight it was irresistible, and even with only two inches of his ten inch length fucking her she begged him to fuck her the whole way, but he held back.

He pushed his cock into the tightest hole he had ever had the pleasure of fucking and reached a tight shield. He pulled back, surging forward to meet it again. He fucked that tight portion of her pussy again and again, stretching her tight cunt. In a frenzy of partial entry he felt his balls seize up and he spurted his hot seed into the shallow cavity of her pussy. He released a huge amount of cum that slid harmlessly off her barrier. He lay on top of her spent. Tearing the shirt from her breasts he began a lazy suckle on one nipple, bringing the pink tip to an erect point of pleasure as she lay beneath him.

It had been the best fucking he had ever done, and yet he had not buried his flesh in hers, not truly fucked her as she ought to have been.

He felt a hand on his back and he was hauled off of the Druid, her legs still spread.

"What have you done? Fool!" Andrew hit Elias and he went careening into the wall. "You need but wait for the ritual to breed her!"

Elias wiped dark blood from his mouth and answered, "She is a virgin, I but went to her barrier."

I watched the dark intent form in the eyes of Andrew.

"Of course!" He smiled at Elias. "She is technically untried but you get a taste of Druid flesh. Brilliant really."

His eyes found mine, then sliding away, he took off his pants and positioned himself above Holly, who in the throes of her first real sexual experience, didn't know how to react.

"No!" I yelled, trying to go to Holly. But Elias was there, holding me back. "Do not interfere. She will be pleasured, you but need watch."

I watched as Andrew put a finger inside Holly, searching for her virginity. Satisfied it was intact, he began to sink his cock inside her.

I watched as her hips rose, encouraging a deeper thrust. The thrust that would threaten to fuck her into non-virginity.

"No you don't, breeder," Andrew said through clenched teeth, there will be time enough to make you ours. He slid in and out, about a third of his cock disappearing as it came out again. He began to move quickly, his movement a blur and murmured, "She's so tight...her flesh grabs mine. It begs for more," he said as he rocked back and forth into her tight snatch.

She grabbed the ass that rode her tight cunt, writhing underneath his thrusts to seek deeper entry, crying out softly while he speared her innocence.

He stiffened above her and came, his body shuddering its release into her pussy. Holly shouted her own release and I could see Andrew's restraint not to shove the rest of his length inside her.

Two more reapers lined up and one said, "I can go the whole way inside her rose bud. I could plant my seed there and my entire cock."

Holly lay with her legs spread, having put her ass up in the air as an offering and the Reaper put his fingers into her pussy, scooping shallowly for the cum he could find then inserting it in her tight bud. He moved his fingers in and out, finally, he replaced his fingers with the blunt tip of his cock. As he inserted his dick slowly into Holly's ass she rose to meet his gentle thrusting. Soon, they had developed a rhythm and Holly was bumping against the whole length of him as he buried his shaft in her virgin ass. He gave another thrust, then one more hard one, groaning as he released his cum in her ass, it puckered and throbbed around his cock, milking him of his juices even as she screamed her orgasm to the room.

The Reaper fell away, sliding a finger inside her tight bud one last time with a sigh.

The last Reaper came behind her and positioning behind her snatch he followed the example of the others before him, making a shallow thrust, he met the resistance of her virginity shield and fucked her to that point.

I could tell that he wanted to plunge deeper, groaning as he met the resistance too soon, but pulling out at just the right time to not breach the barrier. It was no easy thing as Holly didn't act like a virgin, but like a willing slut, throwing her pussy against him even as he pulled away. Finally, he could not stand it and he spilled his hot seed into her hole, much of it sliding out around his prick and her pussy, the lack of full penetration aiding its release.

He rolled Holly over and Elias went to her, leaving me in stunned surprise.

He kneeled between her legs and said, "I will clean you now."

"Yes," she whispered, allowing her knees to fall open, displaying her foamy cunt to Elias, who began lapping at her. He couldn't resist, sinking a finger into her snatch, he moved it back and forth in her flesh and when he thought she was ready and he had cleaned her, he sunk his tongue inside her pussy.

She yelled her pleasure until her throat was raw.

They finished with Holly and without a word, left her cum filled and quaking in the room with me.

They left to hunt.

6

Holly sat straight up in the bed, her hand pressed to her chest, gasping for air.

Her eyes found Rachel's.

It had been a dream.

"Did you have a nightmare?" I asked, watching Holly closely, her face reflecting the way I'd felt earlier when I was torn awake from a sexual liaison beyond any I'd ever known.

She nodded slowly. "They all...took turns on me." She put her face in her hands and cried.

I wrapped my arms around her. We needed to get out of here. The Reapers were pressing their agenda on us. I thought it would get more intense as time went on. Before we knew it, the lines would blur and the dreams would become a reality.

I took Holly's small face in my hands and searched her eyes. "We're gonna have to get out of here, or what you did in the dreams is going to happen. That's what all this dream sharing is about. They had our blood and now they're connected to us. This'll just keep on happening."

"I want Zach. Not them!" she wailed, flinging her arms out.

"Shh...I know, Holly. But it doesn't matter how we feel. That's what I'm trying to tell ya. Because of this god-damned Druid blood, we're like...susceptible or something. To them, the Reapers."

I brushed a tear off her cheek and thought of Cole... and Zach. Where the hell were they? I didn't know if we could escape. They had to sleep but would it be enough? I hung my head, pressing my forehead against Holly's.

Cole and Zach circled the run down motel. The scent of the Druids filled the air all around them.

They were inside those brick and mortar walls, Cole knew it.

"When?" Zach asked impatiently, clenching his huge hands into fists. Fists made for punishment.

"You will have opportunity, my friend," Cole replied, keeping his eyes trained on the building.

"If I know Rachel, she may even now feel our presence. Having taken my blood." Cole kicked a rock and it shot off like a rocket, suddenly angry. What if they had made Rachel have their blood? That would negate her sensitivity to his. Too much speculation, not enough fact.

He did not elaborate to Zach, who was strung taut, his true mate held inside with a quad or more of Reapers in intimate proximity to pure Druids.

A volatile situation to be sure.

Cole focused on the building and pushed his energy, his individualism in a singular pulse toward it. If Rachel was within, she would feel it.

He hoped.

I scrounged around in a closet that had two lone hangers standing at attention on an old wood pole for some kind of bag. If Holly and I were going to leave, we'd need something. Water, blankets? I hit paydirt when I discovered a small trap door at the base of the closet, partially covered by the grossest shag carpeting I'd ever had the bad luck of encountering. Inside of the dark recesses of the cubbyhole was a survival kit. It was definitely from the last world war. It made perfect sense. The building had obviously been a housing establishment for troops then later converted to the seedy motel it became.

I took stock of what was there: 4 glass water bottles, two wool blankets, twelve packs of dehydrated food, and a first aid kit. I chucked that. I figured if I needed first aid, I was already a goner. A grim smile took over my mouth, holding it hostage as I searched and packed.

Finally, Holly asked, "What did ya find?"

I showed her the nearly full backpack and she smiled. "Maybe we can get away." Her expression hopeful.

I looked out at the frozen landscape, picture framed in the glass from the dirty window and sighed. We'd more likely freeze to death than anything.

I opened my mouth to offer weak assurance when I felt it. A warm surge of heat burst in the center of my chest and slid to my extremities in a warm pulse. I gasped. It was the most pleasant and disconcerting sensation I'd ever known. And I knew the source.

Cole.

He was here.

I jerked my head to the door. "Come on! While they're hunting, let's find Zach and Cole.

Holly resisted. "What? What are you talking about?"

I didn't really feel like we had time for me to explain but I said, "I took Cole's blood, he's found us. It's like a beacon. His blood calls to mine."

Holly grabbed the duffel and we flung the cheap motel door open, the first smile of the week on her face.

It faded as she looked into Andrew's face, darkening by the second.

His eyes slid to the duffel, then to mine. "Going somewhere?"

Holly took me at my word and screamed, "Zach!"

And he was there, a blur of muted grays, barreling into Andrew.

That's when all hell broke loose and we watched as a Reaper and *rogue*, took on the foot soldiers of Alexander's kiss.

Cole heard the desperate cry and with barely an acknowledgment, he and Zach triangulated the position and came at Andrew together. Cole allowed Zach to plow into the Reaper while he watched for the others. Where there was one Reaper, there were more.

He was not disappointed as the three that had been melded to the shadowed border of the building came forward. Each one held a weapon of the kiss.

Cole had nothing.

He hazarded a glance behind him and saw the *rogue* was banging the head of a large Reaper against the concrete sidewalk. He had fought beside Andrew in battle. He knew the tenor of the male and girded his loins to kill the other Reapers.

Males he had fought beside.

Cole felt the talons slide out from his fingertips, the usual small stab of pain nothing to what he felt as he walked into certain melee.

Josiah and Elias flanked Cole, one with the preferred curved saber. The ultimate tool for relieving a vampire of their head.

The other had one set of talons in stark relief, moonlight glinting off the polished ivory of them.

Cole did not hesitate, as one who he did not know, came from behind him, he rushed the two Reapers, he slid toward them, using the ice beneath his stout boots for momentum and spun in a twirling spiral, both his hands coming out in front of him. He slashed downward at two targets that were nothing more than a blur of color, but with his acute night vision they slowed before his assault, his talons cutting a path down ribs, sinew, broken and torn flesh.

They fell like mighty trees.

He was too late for what happened next, as the Reaper at his back impaled him with all ten of the talons he had seen silvered in the moonlight.

Cole staggered forward as Rachel screamed, coming for him.

"No!" he barked at her, hoping she would stay back, seek safety. Anything but getting in the middle of battle lust as a Druid female.

He could not think of a worse mix if he had planned it.

Zach saw two of the Reapers fall, and another come from behind Cole. He dropped the Reaper and flew to intercept the one which attacked Cole but was too late.

He hauled the Reaper off Cole and the talons punched their release of his flesh. Rachel threw herself on Cole and he wrapped an arm around her even as his lungs filled with blood.

I saw the Reapers come for Cole even as he slid along the icy ground and propelled himself into a spinning tornado, using the down stroke to slice through the chests of the warriors who came for him. When the one who had been behind Cole, stabbed him with his long claws, I screamed and raced into the heart of the fight, ignoring Cole's harsh warning to flee.

My ass. I wasn't going anywhere, he was hurt and I knew what to do.

My blood would cure his injuries.

As I avoided, by a hair's breadth, the Reaper who grappled with Zach his claw caught my shoulder, and sliced me cleanly. I fell where I stood, the agony so far beyond screaming I fell to the gravel silently, graceful in my pain.

Andrew got on all fours and shook his head. The *rogue* had done his best to make a hole in the concrete with his skull. His gaze slid to his left and he saw his opportunity.

Holly watched Zach rush the Reaper that had stabbed Cole with the worst claws she'd ever seen on anything. She covered her mouth, shock creeping in at the edges of her consciousness and backed away. A small noise made her turn her head but by then it was too late. She was held in an unbreakable embrace.

Andrew's. The one that had sent an orgy to her in a dream.

She screamed and Zach turned to see his soulmate in the arms of a Reaper. The one he had not finished. He took the head of the one he fought almost casually, heaving the body to the ground as he sprinted for Holly.

Holly felt the talon slide against the tender flesh of her throat and felt her bowels clench. She thought she'd known terror before but she hadn't. Not really.

Her eyes met the silvered eyes of Zach and she read many emotions there. But the main one that held true was fear.

Fear for her.

"Stop!" Andrew yelled, taking in the scene of Rachel giving blood to Cole, Josiah and Elias on the ground gasping like salmon out of the sea.

"Do not come further or I will harm the queen!" His glacial eyes blazed out of face gone hard like chiseled granite.

Zach of the *rogue* stopped entirely, stunned into speechlessness.

I took my wrist away from Cole's mouth. He rose to his feet, hauling me up, swaying and lightheaded to my feet.

Had I heard Andrew right?

Cole tucked me underneath his arm and dragged me to where Andrew stood.

"What are you saying?" Cole asked, then added, "Do not hurt Holly. You of all vampire understand her value."

Andrew face showed a wash of different emotions. Finally the right one took residence on his expression. He slowly released Holly and she rushed to Zach where they crashed into each other. He rained kisses all over her face, while murmuring soft words to her.

Zach turned Holly into his body and watched as the wounded Reapers rose to their feet and gave Cole a look.

Cole was not wholly steady but one look at Andrew told him he was in charge of the Reapers who approached. Their gaping slash wounds began to close even as he watched.

The group made an uneasy truce and went into the large suite the Reapers had procured through compulsion. Finally, after much situating the three Reapers who lived faced off with Cole and Zach.

Andrew pointed at Zach and said, "This one may not understand or be privy to the law. The ancient order. But you, Cole. You understand much."

Cole sighed. He thought he knew what all this meant and he pulled Rachel closer to his body. He never thought he would have seen this day come.

He nodded. "It is possible. But…"

"Unbelievable," Andrew supplied.

Cole nodded.

Holly looked out from the circle of protection of Zach's strong arms. "What? Why are you all looking at me?"

"Tell her if you like. She has already been involved in the mating ceremony through dream share." He looked at Holly significantly and she blushed a deep red.

Zach growled low in his throat. He knew what a dream share was. That they would have mated with the one that was meant for him was beyond apology.

He put Holly behind his back and moved toward Andrew.

"Wait, friend," Cole instructed Zach.

"Why should I?" he said without turning. "This one has admitted that they violated Holly while she slept."

Cole looked at Zach, his body poised for violence, his hands clenched and ready to beat and pound.

Zach turned and regarded Cole.

Cole spread his hands and began the telling of the ancient vampire prophesy.

"Centuries ago, in the Book of Prophesy…"

"The Book of Blood?" Zach asked.

Cole nodded. "If you like that name."

Zach went back to Holly, throwing a scathing glance at Andrew behind him.

"In any event, it promised that there would come a pure blood Druid, a virgin. And when she was bred by one not accepted…"

"*Rogue*," Josiah said in a low voice.

Cole continued, "Then she would serve three others. From this singular event, she would sire kings. Vampire kings that would be daywalkers. All the good of vampire, but without the disability of walking only by the moon."

"That cannot be!" Zach seethed, looking at a scared Holly.

"I am sorry, Zach. Taken with the presence of Rachel…" Cole began.

"What do I have to do with all this prophesy crap?" I asked. As if there weren't enough things to keep me pissed off. Finally, I was reunited with Cole after what seemed like one long nightmare of running only to find out Holly was some kind of whacked out Vamp Queen. *No.*

Cole chuckled. "Rachel, the prophesy tells of two Druid women who are kin. That the older will guide the younger. She will be the confidant to the queen. A helpmate of sorts."

I was Holly's sister? I mean...I'd noticed the resemblance but no way. I was adopted, there were no other relatives. I told them that. Vehemently denying relation.

"I was adopted too," Holly said.

We looked at each other.

Elias and Josiah said in unison, "Protection."

"What?" I asked harshly, my hands planted on my hips.

Elias came forward and I scooted back a little toward Cole. He stopped moving. "We have spoken much and think that there is a contingent of Druids that know of our kind. Actively seeking secrecy by hiding pure offspring."

"Okay, say that's true. Then where are all the others?"

Cole interjected, "They may be breeding themselves. Keeping things quiet."

"But that doesn't make sense," Holly said. "If I was so important then why would they give me up?" She swiped a tear away and Zach curled his massive body around her protectively.

"They may not have known. It was probably the best contingency they had. There may be more 'soulmates' amongst those pure Druids that are hidden from us. More that could be with their vampire mates. If it were not for this faction," Andrew elaborated.

"What does this mean for me?" Holly asked, pleading for an answer that wouldn't be what she thought it might.

"To be perfectly blunt, the arms that hold you are the ones you will reside in. But you are destined to be the mother of vampirekind. For that outcome, this one must claim your virginity, then allow the three of us to spill our seed within the ripeness of your womb, sealing your destiny forever."

Holly looked at them in horror.

When Elias saw her expression he said, "Was the dream share really that awful?"

Holly's face became red as Zach said, "What if I do not want to share her? My one true mate?"

"What if your sons could be daywalkers? Vampires of the sun?" Josiah asked, brows to his hairline.

Zach was quiet for a heartbeat, thinking of the enormity of what that meant for their race.

Cole spoke up, his voice ringing with finality, "I have not said the last."

All eyes were on him.

"The queen will begin a new coven, a coven of one who is not Reaper, the rest will be of Reaper bloodline. And most importantly, the Book says that she shall be as a beacon to other Druids, her light casting a call of such brilliance and sound, that all will answer."

The room lay silent.

Holly was overwhelmed and put her head in her hands.

I was pretty sure when she'd gone to study group a few months ago, she'd never planned on being a queen.

Queen of the vampire.

safe

The house was old and drafty, roomy.

But the vampires warmed our chilled flesh.

I hadn't really gotten used to where we were yet. Not running, living a life that seemed like a dream. Even with as modern as I thought I was, the Reapers, and Zach, had an ancient logic, which they applied.

The house stood above Seattle, the city buildings and their twinkling lights winking back at us as we worked in the kitchen, Holly and I.

She cut vegetables that only we would eat. I sliced the tender cut of meat into long strips that would stir fry up into the fajita mix they'd become.

Holly paused in cutting, looking at me over the steam from the frying pan, butter and an aromatic mix of spices wafting through the kitchen, rising to the ten foot ceilings above. "I'm scared," she said, using the knife to slide the remainder of the veggies off the wooden cutting board and

MARATA EROS

into the pan. It sizzled as it made blunt contact with the buttery heat.

I turned, placing a hand on my hip. I lifted a shoulder in a half shrug. "I trust Cole. They didn't traverse a frozen landscape of two thousand miles if they weren't serious." I searched her eyes.

"I had a plan, Rachel. A life!" Holly said in a loud huff.

I thought of my life in the cubicle, my cat, my stuff... it just seemed so long ago. Had I been happy? I thought... I'd been content. That was the most accurate assessment of my former life I could make. But how to convey that to a nineteen-year old woman.

A woman that was actually my sister.

I felt my face soften. "I understand. Nine years ago I was your age. I had the world by the testies." I squeezed my hand into a fist and Holly giggled, turning to stir the meal into cooperative completion.

"But," I spoke to her back, her hair a black sweep between her shoulder blades. "It wasn't some great adulthood. I had a best friend that was superficial and we were looking for different things. I had a job I could barely stand..." I let my sentence trail off. "*Here* we are unique. In *this* life, with the vampire, we matter for what we are in a way that others can't. We have purpose." I smiled suddenly, feeling the caress of one of my deep dimples. "And then there is the lifespan advantage!"

Holly glowered. Taking the food and pouring it into a bowl, I then loaded the tortillas with the guts of the meal, ladling a spoonful of sour cream and salsa. *Perfect*, I thought, watching the colorful goodness of orange and red peppers steam on our waiting plates.

We sat down on the bar stools by the elevated breakfast bar as Holly picked at her food. "I don't know if I wanna live forever. I don't know if I want to be a queen. I'm nineteen. A few months ago the most I had to consider was what class to sign up for." She swiped a tear that had fallen, threatening to land on her food.

I folded my hands. "Listen, I know this is really overwhelming but this is what it is. If we believe what the vampire say about the prophesy, the Druid lineage, all of it, then, this is where we were meant to be. And believe me, I'd rather be with these dudes than that creepy Alexander."

Holly shuddered, thinking about the stories I'd told about my short stay in that coven. "There would've been no choice there. Free will, gone. Here, you will be a queen. You will be respected and they'll be devoted to you."

"I just want Zach," Holly said flatly.

"Okay, so it's not so hot that they all have to have sex with you for this," I put my fingers up and made air quotes, 'ritual of royalty'. But, it could be worse. Even Zach has conceded it." I stared into her eyes, so like my own it was eerie. "It doesn't mean he's not doing the alpha male jig and having big cows and stuff."

Holly laughed despite herself, sticking her first mouthful of food in her craw and chewing thoughtfully.

"Look at it as a task you have to accomplish," I said with mirth. I held up my hand and started ticking off the points, "You have to have sex with four males. The first one, your soul mate, will take your virginity. Then each subsequent male will grovel before you sexually, doing all in their power to bring you to orgasm, while you watch their hotness in the throes of passion." I laughed and continued, "I think it may be something you can bear?"

That got the grin out of her I was hoping for.

"I'm scared," she said again.

"They won't hurt you, obviously."

"I know, but I've heard..." she began.

"It is," I answered for her. "But that only lasts a little while and they'll be priming the pump, so to speak." I grinned and she returned it.

"You'll see," I said, scooping the juices that were running out of the tortilla and taking a messy bite. We looked at each other as we ate, then I looked at the clock.

Time was moving toward the big ritual. Holly a virgin no more.

For me, I was quaking with anticipation of finally being bonded forever to Cole.

8

Queen

Holly looked resplendent in her flowing gown of white. Josiah, Elias, Andrew and her true mate, Zach, stood in front of her.

It was like a weird wedding. But, unlike other weddings, this felt more real and right than any I'd ever attended.

We'd spent hours in a bath, talking and getting Holly ready. After trying a million different hairstyles, in the end, simple had been the order of the day and Holly looked perfect, blue highlights shining in the sweep of raven-colored hair that graced her body, falling nearly to her waist.

Zach came to her and took her hands, Cole presided. In his grip was a thick book, darkened to a deep bronze with age.

He began, reciting a ceremony designed to give the Vampire hope. A species separate from humans, but forced to live among them. At the top of a food chain that was too great in number to conquer and too necessary to exterminate.

When he finished Zach took Holly's face in his hands, giving her a chaste kiss, cradling her head like a fragile egg. She pressed her body against his, the blackness of his attire in sharp contrast to the whiteness of hers. He wrapped her in his arms and, picking her up in a classic cradle hold he strode to their matrimony chamber.

Holly was more nervous than she'd ever been in her whole life. She sat on the edge of the bed as Zach turned the lock. She had completely put the Reapers that she'd have to share her body with before long out of her mind. Right now, she was concentrating on the male that would give her pleasure.

The *rogue*.

Warmth pooled in the junction between her thighs and she scissored them together subtly as he drew near.

Zach laughed low in his throat. "It is normal for you to become aroused with my nearness."

Holly blushed. There were no secrets either. He could smell her arousal, her eagerness.

Zach crawled across the bed taking his large palm and pressing it to the back of her neck, drawing her face close to his. His lips hovered over hers, his breath cinnamon and spice.

Consumable.

When he closed their flesh in an embrace of lips that slid into tongues, Holly's breath came short and fast. Zach undressed her before she was even aware of it, her gown at her waist and her breasts falling out like ripe globes with erect pink tips. Zach didn't let them beg for attention but blazed a trail of kisses from her swollen mouth and wrapped his lips around the sensitive nipple, suckling it until Holly moaned with desire, her hips wiggling underneath where his lay in the cradle of her body.

He took her moan for the invitation it was and tore the gown off the rest of the way, settling his nakedness against her core, the hot folds of flesh already wet with her honey, waiting for his final entry.

But he took his time. Zach did not wish for her first time to be a rushed affair. He settled in between her thighs, releasing her nipple with an abrupt pop that left her gasping, the cooler air of the room teasing it to hard erectness. Zach let one hand ride that hard point while the other began to work the bud between her folds, the pleasure button opening like a subtle flower, the sweet fragrance of her filling his senses, making his head spin with the exquisiteness of her.

She was made for him, all of her, and he for her. From the top of her head to her pinky toe and Zach was determined to make the most of it.

"Please..." Holly began. "Please put your finger in me..." she grabbed his hair with her fingers, pushing his face down until his tongue had replaced his finger and he began a slow pull and suck of her clit, her hips pressing a rhythm in his face that made him growl his pleasure against her glistening secret flesh. He did what she asked and after feeling the maidenhead of her innocence resist the blunt end of his finger he plunged his finger just shy of breaching that tender barrier. When she thrust her hips to receive him more deeply, he inserted a second finger and pushed and pulled while his tongue worked circular magic against her sensitive nub.

Holly felt herself building toward a liquid release. When the wave of pleasure reached to the shore of her body, she shouted into the stillness of the room, the moment transcending any physical pleasure she'd ever experienced. Her knees fell open and with languid respite, she watched Zach as he positioned himself above her and began to guide the blunt head of himself inside her untested entrance, made wet by his attentions.

When Zach reached her barrier he looked into her eyes, upon seeing the invitation light their depths, he surged inside her.

Holly gasped at the pleasure/pain sensation as his shaft rocked into the tightness of her wet channel and surged through her resistance. The accordion-like flesh pulled against him as he slowly withdrew. She could feel the slide of him and the erotic pleasure he could give her as she relaxed into his sensuous rhythm, matching it with her own.

Zach felt her relax against the soft assault of their flesh meeting and rocked inside her again, the third thrust putting him against the entrance to her womb. His cock throbbing with the need to release he pulled out and seeking her acceptance he said, "Please, I need to…"

Holly nodded, she knew what he wanted and she was ready, the initial piercing of her pussy melting away into constant pleasure as his prick stabbed her hot core, the tightness of it a velvet glove on his shaft.

Zach began a light punish of her pussy, thrusting deep, pulling out and continuing, he pressed up on his hands, his shoulder muscles bunching as he began to hammer into her and she met him with each thrust.

Holly could feel that delicious throbbing pulse.

Once.

Twice.

Zach thrust deeply a third time, shuddering as his hot seed poured into a pussy that exploded around his shaft, each pulse stronger than the last, sucking the seed from deep inside his prick.

Without pulling out he collapsed on top of her softly, tucking her in against him, their flesh still married head to hip. Her softness melding with the hard length of him.

Zach squeezed his queen's face against his chest and closed his eyes, having never felt a synchronicity as complete as this moment held for him.

9

Cole undressed Rachel with barely contained relish. Finally, he would consummate a relationship he had yearned for his entire vampiric lifetime. After months of running and strife, they had found a place to be, to exist together. A new order of coven, where Druid and Reaper flesh could unite to form a new race.

I couldn't wait for his touch and pushed the black leather from his massive shoulders. Cole shrugged it off, tearing his belt through loops with a high, whistling sound, the only noise in the room.

He tore the black T-shirt over his head, no hair to get in the way of his nakedness, the skull trim a shadow of black on his head as he dipped forward to capture my lips in his.

I melted into the hard lines of his body, never resisting, beyond resistance.

Cole carried me to the bed, pushing up the formal skirt I had worn to the "wedding" of the new queen.

My Druid sister.

To mate with me all Cole needed to do was plunge his shaft into me, spilling his Reaper's seed deep in my channel to ignite a pregnancy that would begin the new race. A race of equality and happiness. I didn't want to think about what it would mean to other vampire that there were Reapers and Druids pairing off and breeding out the low vampire. Leaving the old ways behind.

Cole growled and my distracted attention went back to what he was doing. "I cannot give you the pleasure I would wish for you, Rachel. I must bury myself like a sword of flesh in your body and spill my seed," he said, his voice strained as he saw my panties, sheer enough to see the small *V* of hair that grew there revealed to perfection through the hot scarlet fabric.

He bent low and tore the panties off with his fangs, the pull of the fabric jerking my body. Cole immediately plunged his face into my pussy, his fangs out and rubbing delicately along first one fold then the other, like a cat scent-marking, he rubbed until my moistened honey poured out of my hot hole.

"You are so ready," he murmured against the heat of my snatch. He put his large hands on my thighs and gently spread them until my folds were spread and pink, open for his sensual invasion.

I opened my legs further, inviting the exploration of his fingers. Cole complied by inserting two fingers, slipping them in and out until my breathing came fast and hard. I felt like I was hyperventilating.

"Put it in me...please!" I said in a hoarse voice, I couldn't stand it anymore. So many times interrupted, so many delays. I wanted his prick in me as deep as it would go. I spread my legs and lifted my hips even as I felt his finger leave me and the tip of his huge cock widen my opening to accommodate his size.

Which was considerable.

Cole worked his prick in, spreading the tightness of me until his entire length was buried to the end of me. He slowly pulled out, my pussy grabbing at him the whole way. I'd never been with a man that felt this way, this tantalizing dance of flesh perfectly matched, fully attuned to each other's bodies.

I moved to meet him and as he began to plunge in and out of me, smoothly pulling out and entering deeply I could feel the heat from his thrusts build inside my core, the need to release a deafening rhythm that only he could relieve, a delicious roaring in my ears.

"Rachel," Cole said, his dark eyes meeting mine, no longer silver in the low light of the room. "Look at me as I spill my seed into your willing vessel."

I did, falling into the well of eyes gone obsidian with desire, intent.

I lifted and he plunged. Finally, our flesh smacking together...it stuck and he grew still above me.

Then I felt it, a warmth spread deep within my pussy, hot seed filling me, my legs spread to receive, my pussy open to accept. I could feel my pulses as an orgasm shattered in response to his cum, sucking every bit of what he was giving deep within me.

With his prick still throbbing inside my pulsating pussy he said, "And now, I will pleasure you."

He withdrew from the center of my pleasure, his face, tongue and hands descending on my wet and satisfied core.

He buried his face in me.

We stayed that way for a long while.

While I writhed beneath him in an ecstasy beyond measure.

10

I laughed alongside Holly. We were *so* into a routine, pleasing our vampire mates at rest and frolicking during the day. Protected, fulfilled and no longer dissatisfied with our meager existences from before.

"I'm not bowlegged!" Holly mock huffed, her hands crossed and cradling a bosom that was well displayed in the clothing that Zach liked to see her in.

"I don't know, you spend more time in your bedroom than out of it!" I laughed.

Holly looked down at the spoon in her hand and blushed a light pink, the color spreading across her cheekbones delicately. "That's true, but you're one to talk! We can hear you and Cole from two states away!"

I smiled, she had me there. "Wait until more Druids come…this will turn into a pleasure palace."

"I think it already is," Holly said with a smirk.

I smiled, thinking she'd come a long way from innocent virgin to willing queenly slut. But not quite yet. She was due to consummate with the three Reapers.

Cole and I were mated and her true mate had enjoyed unlimited access to her willing body for a week.

As I thought of it The Natives were Restless.

In this case, the vampire.

As if on cue, Josiah, Elias and Andrew entered the room, their eyelids at half-mast, all attention on Holly.

She was feeling the moment, I could tell. She stood, smoothing a hand over her long skirt, the material had a metallic thread running throughout, in gold. Fit for a queen. A bustier in a deep crimson, tied and cinched, accentuated her wasp waist while heaving her ample breasts to be displayed like ripe plums for the taking.

The males watched her move toward them and met her halfway across the room.

"I'm ready," she breathed as each one began to seductively paw her as she stood there.

"We know," Andrew said.

"We smell your fertility; you are ripe to accept our seed within you," Josiah told her.

Elias buried his hand beneath her skirt. Her soft moaning told me all I needed to know about where his finger had disappeared to.

Josiah and Andrew picked her up as Elias caressed and plundered her hidden flesh.

Holly's eyes met mine as the Reapers carried her away.
To fuck her into oblivion.
Or bliss.
No, I thought…*definitely bliss.*

The Druid Series is available in two paperback volumes, plus Druids 7-9!

Read on for the exciting first chapter of **TDS 4: Sow....**

THE
DRUID
SERIES 4
SOW

AUTHOR OF
A TERRIBLE LOVE

MARATA
NEW YORK TIMES & USA TODAY BESTSELLING AUTHOR
EROS

SOW

The Druid Series 4

Copyright © 2012 Marata Eros

Edited by Hazel Novak

DEDICATION:

For my husband,
without whom, these stories would not exist:
His encouragement has meant everything.

1

Rachel was going a little stir crazy. The boys were so overprotective they couldn't even shop, except at night with them accompanying, of course. She remembered exactly the conversation she'd had with Cole.

"Please," she gazed up at him, giving him the Big Time Big Eye. That's code for puppy dog eyes-given-by-a-chick. It was generally pretty effective. Add in a dash of sex and it cinched the deal.

Usually.

Cole scrubbed a frustrated hand over the top of his skull trim, shifting his weight, the subtle crackling of the leather the only noise in the quiet of their bedroom. He looked down at Rachel and knew he was weak to her requests.

Except when it came to this. He would not risk her safety, and for fucking groceries? Not happening.

Cole shook his head even as she pressed herself against him and he felt himself harden at her nearness. He answered with his lips, his tongue. Dragging Rachel against him, he used one large palm to press her face against his mouth and the other hand at her lower back.

Rachel groaned inside the luscious cavity of Cole's mouth, his fangs a smooth and erotic press against her tender lip as he nipped. The minutest amount of blood escaped and Cole hissed, sucking her lip into his mouth, caressing the small wound with his mouth as he kneaded her ass. Hauling Rachel up one-handed she responded by wrapping her legs around his waist and in a smooth motion he turned her and laid her on the bed.

Cole looked at Rachel. Her black hair was spread like a silken fan of water around her, outlining the silhouette of her body to perfection. Cole took a moment to gaze at this Druid woman he now claimed as life mate, her age arrested in this space of time, twenty-eight forever.

"What?" Rachel breathed out, already opening her legs at the knee to show him what waited for him.

She very well knew what she did to him. He smiled in a slow seductive grin. "You know what you do…" Cole leaned forward, his leather clad knee pressed against the mound of feminine flesh that was firmly encased in panties so sheer they could not claim to be actual material.

"Does this mean Holly and I can go out?" Rachel asked, using a slim and tapered finger to work the panties lower until the top of her delectable slit peaked out from the scalloped edge.

Cole swallowed, his cock throbbing to be put to use. With a supreme effort he answered around the searing heat of his arousal, his need to spear her with his sword of flesh a weight upon his body, "Not without human guards."

Rachel pouted, "We're bored, Cole. We can't stay like prisoners all the time in this big house."

Rachel's eyes widened at his expression.

"Bored, eh?" Cole growled and Rachel squealed at the sound he made in his throat.

He fell on her softly, tearing off the panties he had admired but moments before.

With his fangs.

Cole thought he could take care of some of her boredom.

Beau

Beau made his way down the cobblestoned alley of the back of the bistro he worked at, his mouth on fire. He moved his jaw gingerly from side to side, it'd been this way for months. Every joint on damn fire, his mouth was the fucking worst. He'd been to a doctor; lot of fat goddamned good that did. They couldn't figure out what his problem was and Beau wasn't about to spend the whole shitty health care deductible on tests that yielded nothing. The bistro wouldn't give him the hours he needed for the better health care. He was lucky to have any crummy job. After all, who'd hire him?

Given the fact that he had no past.

No social security card, no effing last name.

Just Beau.

That was all the memory he had. It was like he'd been robbed. Of his life.

A light drizzle fell, pressing his dark hair against his forehead like a damp helmet and Beau thought about how he'd landed in the gray depths of Seattle. Where he'd come from. What it meant.

Same endless circle of questions that never got answered, always swirling like an irritating merry-go-round that never stopped.

His introspection was shattered like brittle glass when he heard a woman screaming. At the same time a surging wakefulness of adrenaline kicked in, causing him to be momentarily dizzy. He slapped his palm against the cold brick of the alley building and steadied himself.

What the fuck was this? The inside of Beau's mouth throbbed in time to his heartbeat and there was a liquid pain filling his joints as he stood there.

There was pain…but underneath that there was something else that swam just outside of it:

Power.

Beau ignored the oddities of his body and charged toward the frightened sounds of a female in trouble.

THE
DARA
NICHOLS
A HARD LESSON
SERIES
1

NEW YORK TIMES & USA TODAY BESTSELLING AUTHOR

MARATA EROS

AUTHOR OF *A TERRIBLE LOVE*

*A **free** short erotic story*

1

Dara Nichols had her back to the class, writing an outline for *Essential Essay Writing*, when she heard the whispering. Whirling around, on the defensive, she saw it was the same group of young men that it always was.

She sighed. Ryan, Kevin, Jason and Sean sat in a loose huddle of desks and stared at her, heat in their eyes. *Again*.

Dara was tired of it. She got it, duh…she was the quintessential, "older woman," in a position of authority, a professor of English in a prestigious college, so why did that group of guys have to ogle her every day? They wouldn't give any effort and she wasn't going to pass their asses just because their parents were paying top-coin for a pricey college education. There were plenty of women their own age that would beg to screw them. Why pick on her?

They could, by God, tone it right-the-fuck down.

The rub was that they made her wet with their attentions. She hated that she couldn't be one hundred percent

263

professional with them around, tracking her every move with their eyes.

Much to her shame, she had started dressing to gain more attention, not less. Her skirts shorter, her blouses hotter, her thigh-highs silkier, *lacier*. She had always loved heels but she had added platforms to her ensemble and was ranging at almost six feet tall when she had those babies on. Which was most of the time now.

Today, she'd elected not to wear panties. There was nowhere for the moisture of her arousal to go and it made her thighs slick as she moved back and forth in front of the white board. In front of their hot gazes, she prowled in front of them, untamed and hot, ready for anything.

2

Dara survived the lecture, her hair coming loose from the messy bun, stabbed through by a glittering hair stick that she always wore at the college. Her administrator frowned on wearing her hair down. And she had a lot of it. At forty, she realized that her deep auburn hair, cascading almost to her waist, was a nod to her waning youth but she still looked good, worked out, didn't have a battalion of wrinkles...so, she wore it long.

Her head was bowed as she leaned over her desk, grabbing papers, organizing, recycling some and stacking others to put in her briefcase...when a large hand came down on the stack in front of her.

She looked up and it was Ryan. She liked to think of him as the ringleader. The one that always had a wisecrack when she pressed him for an answer...a legitimate answer. She couldn't nail him on outright rudeness and inappropriate behavior. Oh no, not him, he rode that fine line between what he knew would get him nailed and what would get him noticed.

Dara was noticing.

She straightened, arching her back slightly and he looked at the lacy cami she wore under her low cut top. A lock of hair fell forward and she moved to put it behind her ear and he touched the strand, fingering it, then gently put it behind her ear.

Dara stepped away from the intimate touch, "Not appropriate, Ryan."

Ryan turned to the rest of the guys standing there and said, "Hit the lock."

Her heart sped, she belatedly realized that this was her last class and all the rest of her students had left soundlessly through the solid wood door, thoughts of the weekend stretched before them.

"Don't touch that," she said in a breathy voice.

Kevin, a six-foot three, muscular, football scholarship student ignored her, turning the dead bolt lock and Dara jumped as it snapped into place.

Coming to her senses, she rounded the desk, her heels clicking on the hard floor, dimly realizing that Jason was systematically closing all the blinds on the windows which faced the outside.

Holy shit, she thought.

Sean grabbed her from behind with strong arms and she yelped in surprise, his height exactly matched hers, the smell of spice and soap came through her fog of shock.

This couldn't be happening to her. She was a professional, these were her students, she had never come on to them, been inappropriate...

Ryan walked toward her, six-foot two, lean fighting machine, black hair and brown eyes the color of root beer, "We've been watching you, *Ms. Nichols*. That tight ass of yours back-and-forth," he made a sweeping motion with his finger, "in front of us...teasing us. We know about older women, they're not like girls our age."

Sean, who still had his arms wrapped around her waist, whispered in her ear, "We don't study English, but we've been reading. We know you're in your sexual prime, you move like you were born to screw..."

Jason had finished with the blinds and got down on his knees in front of her legs, his face inches from the hem of her skirt, the lace of her stockings peeking out from beneath it, "We're not rapists..."

"Not that we couldn't give it to you rough," Ryan said, his hazel eyes as serious as she'd ever seen them.

This couldn't be happening, they meant to take her, right here, in her classroom where she taught English! And her pussy was engorged and wet, just weeping for one of them and she was ashamed anew.

"I'm sorry..." she stammered, "I didn't mean to give you guys the wrong impression..."

Jason continued as if she had never spoken, "Say the word and we'll go. Tell us you don't want our cocks buried in all your holes."

"Your mouth," Kevin said.

"Your tight ass," Sean leaned close to her ear seductively.

"And especially your honeypot," Ryan said.

She couldn't help it, she moaned and they moved in. Jason ran a hand up her thigh, the golden hairs of his arm disappearing out of sight as he put his hand underneath her skirt and his finger pushed its way inside her sopping cunt.

"Oh God, she's soaking wet! And, no panties!" Jason said with barely contained joy.

She couldn't let this happen and began to close her legs and his finger came out, "We won't force you, but you're slick and wet and ready to get fucked. Just let me taste you and if you still don't want to, we can go."

Dara answered by spreading her legs, the feel of that one finger having slipped into her wet hole more than she could bear. Sean pulled her backward across the desk, his arms looped behind and underneath her arms, effectively pinning her.

Jason dropped his face into her smooth pussy and lapped at each side of her labia while his finger fucked her and she moaned her pleasure, pushing her hips closer to his tongue.

"Stuff your cock in her mouth!" Sean said, his voice vibrating with urgency.

Suddenly Kevin was there, eyes she'd looked into a hundred times, full of a dark possession. He put the thick head of his cock above her lips and she opened her mouth to accept what he gave her, saliva filling it, as he started to slide it in and out of her mouth, matching the rhythm of Jason's fingers fucking her. She reached up and cupped his balls, massaging them while running a slim finger under the delicate underside that traveled to his ass.

"God...look at her all spread and wet, taking the cock, taking the fingers," Ryan said. "Make her come and then I want to pound that snatch and spray my cum up there."

Just thinking of getting fucked by them all, made the pressure build in her cunt and she racketed up to a frenzy, her orgasm boiling out of her snatch and making her shove her hips hard into Jason's seeking tongue, and he responded by burying his face in her pussy. Kevin suddenly went rigid above her, all but making her gag, "Swallow my cum you slut..."and she did; it was swallow or choke. It was such a turn-on that she lay there spent, licking her lips as Jason came into view.

"I...what?" she began.

"You want it, don't you?" Ryan said and Sean let go behind her and she fell back as Jason took his place, cradling her upper body as he began to undo her blouse, each button popping to reveal her lacy black cami and bra, swollen nipples poking through the lace like erotic pebbles.

They waited for Dara to say the word and she did, "Yes," she breathed out. She couldn't wait to fulfill the subconscious fantasy she'd entertained when they had begun performing visual foreplay with her each day.

Ryan dropped his jeans and underwear in a pool by his ankles, taking a cock in his hand that was easily ten inches, his fingers not meeting its girth.

Dara shook her head, "I can't take that much.." Yet, more moisture bloomed in her pussy by the mere thought all that cock in her tight hole.

Jason shoved his cock into her mouth and she felt Ryan exploring her opening with his fingers, gauging what he thought she could manage.

"She's got a tight pussy, it'll feel good on my pole. Spread your legs, Ms. Nichols," he said with an edge of sarcasm.

"Hold her down, open her legs farther, I need to work this into her," Ryan grunted, starting to put the blunt tip of the biggest cock she'd ever taken in her. He worked it in, each inch a battle. It stretched her so wide, she groaned as Jason mouth-fucked her, it felt so good to be stretched to her limit. She couldn't tell him to slow down or that she was too tight because her mouth was full of cock, which made it hotter.

"Oh, God, she's so tight but so wet," he said. Reaching the end of her, he pulled out slowly and her channel rippled in response, latching on with a pre-orgasmic pulse, as her body tightened in response to the cock stuffed in her and she made a muffled cry.

All finesse lost, he began thrusting into her snatch in earnest, the shaft going in and out and it shattered Dara, that huge horse cock taking her, stretching her pussy to the point of tearing. "She's wet like a whore but tight like a virgin," he said, his hands pinned on either side of her hips, pounding her into the table while Jason leaned forward, his balls hitting her face as he fucked her mouth.

"That's it...take it all in," he grabbed a handful of her hair and the hair-stick went flying to the floor where it skittered under the desk. He turned her head so he could look into her eyes, "I'm going to come and you're going to swallow it."

She nodded and as he was coming in her mouth he gave one final, deep thrust, howling, "Fuck, yeah!" and she felt the warm spray of his release deep inside her simultaneously with Ryan, her pussy exploding with plea- sure as it pulsated around Ryan's cock. They slowed their rhythm, and finally pulled out as her finger went to her opening to feel what was leaking out of her while spreading it around like lubricant.

"Next," Ryan said, wiping the sweat off his face, giving her nipple an appreciative squeeze and jamming a finger in her pussy to feel his cum in her snatch, and she caught her breath from the force of the finger, "Yeah, I got a good load in there for you dudes to skate right in."

Dara lay there in a pool of satisfied arousal. She'd had two students blast their cum in her mouth and one in her pussy and still she felt like she could be used more.

Sean walked over, cock in hand and said, "My patience is up, guys. I am fucking her in her pussy then her ass."

Dara said, "No, not ass, I've never had a cock there."

"You're gonna have one today," Sean said.

Her pussy got wet thinking about it, but what if she couldn't do it? She thought of Ryan's huge cock. She glanced to her left and Kevin was already hard again, shrugging, "I'm twenty-two, I could get hard twice more if I need to, and I want to fuck your pussy too. And maybe that sweet, tight ass I've seen in skirts for three months…"

"Yeah," Sean said, finger-fucking her pussy. "Nice job Ryan, it's like lube, but better. Wonder how much cum we can get in here?"

"Let's find out," Jason said, his neatly trimmed red pubic hair riding over the cock she'd sucked first, standing at attention and ready to go again.

Ryan drew near her face, "Let's get you on your hands and knees and we can do you that way and you suck me off."

Dara could hardly move, having been fucked by that huge cock and face-fucked by Kevin and then Jason.

Ryan smiled, "We'll help you, *teacher.*"

They moved her limbs into position and took off everything but her thigh-highs and crimson heels. She threw her ass up in the air like an offering and spread her legs, no longer caring that they were all almost twenty years younger than her, that she was their teacher.

She just wanted all her holes filled with cum.

Sean moved up behind her, bumping her ass with his engorged cock, driving it into her cum-filled hole as Ryan shoved her face down on his cock. They began to move in a rhythm of fucking her; Sean pulling out, and Ryan shoving her mouth down his shaft, slick with the cum from the men before him.

As Sean thrust his cock in again, "You're right, she is so tight and wet, and your cum is leaking out of her. Nice," and he slapped her ass. She moaned and he did it again, sliding a finger into her ass as he did and an orgasm made her writhe and buck underneath him, shoving her ass against him so she could take more of the finger he was grinding in her ass as his prick speared her pussy.

Ryan made her gag, he was simply to big for her but he pounded the back of her throat anyway and as Sean was coming in her pussy, his finger buried in her ass, Ryan fisted a hand in her hair and slammed her face down to the base of him and came. She choked and gagged, her reflex making her jerk back but he held her there, leaning in close to her he said, "Swallow it, swallow it…."

She came hard as she swallowed, her trembling legs involuntarily spreading wider.

Sean withdrew from her pussy, and Ryan's cock exited her mouth, cum leaving a thin trail on the desk, she lay there with her legs spread for the next man, her pussy pulsating from the last orgasm, burning to be taken again.

"Look at that…" Ryan said. "Never had a woman take the whole load before," he said with satisfaction, grabbing her tits, he mounded them up hard and took a nipple into his mouth, sucking and licking it.

"Please stop, it's too much, I almost couldn't breath with that," Dara said, with tears filling her eyes. It had been great but then it got to be so overwhelming.

"Think she's losing her nerve, guys," Jason said, a raging hard on in his grip.

Ryan said, just inches from her face, "You need to relieve us all. You need to finish what we started," and he straightened. "I plan to have that ass. All of us want to finish and say we had all your holes, and that's what's gonna happen."

His domination over her was the hottest part of it and Dara wanted to do more, feel more.

He walked over to the group, "Spread her legs again, fuck her good and then we go in one at a time and pump that gorgeous ass full of cum."

Dara put up her hand, "I don't think I can. I've never done this before. This many guys. I've never done more than one guy."

Ryan strode over to where she lay and stuck a finger in her pussy, and she sucked in her breath at how good the intrusion felt, "Your mouth says 'I don't know' and your pussy says 'fuck me and fill me'." He put another finger in her and started a slow in and out pull, then added a third and she groaned and gyrated her hips against his hand while he smiled.

"You've had two guys come in you and your pussy is weeping for more. Listen," in and out his fingers went and her snatch was latching onto his fingers for dear life, making a sucking sound of pleasure.

"You've got the sluttiest pussy I've ever fucked and it'll just get better and better with use. Now spread those gorgeous legs like the slut you are and let these guys bang you."

Dara let her legs fall open again as her hole dripped with cum from Ryan and Sean. Jason began to dig in, thrusting his cock in her now-dripping hole, the cum all mixed up with her juices, her body moving on the desk again, his hands wrapped around her ankles as he pressed his advantage.

Suddenly, he pulled out and flipped her over and her stomach was on the desk and her ass spread and open. He gave one, two and with a final deep thrust he tore out of her pussy. He started shoving his cock into her ass, where it burned, but her hole took more than she thought it would. The sensation was wonderful as another orgasm began to build.

"I knew fucking her would be awesome. Keep your ass open, ah-yeah, like that," Dara spread her legs as far as they would go and felt Jason pumping his shaft into her ass, as her hips rose to meet his cock. His rhythm increased, filling her nether regions and a shattering orgasm pushed her ass against his cock and he sprayed his load into her ass, yelling, "Fuck yeah! Ah, it's all in there."

Her pussy was pulsing and her ass felt hot and used but the next man was ready to mount her, "Get me lube. I don't want a dry ass."

It was Kevin. She recognized his voice.

"Fuck her first. There's plenty of cum in there to use."

And he did. Using his cock and making her moan her pleasure as he went about a third of the way in, slowly pulling out, then stabbing it in the whole way. The sensation was exquisite.

"Oh yeah…she likes that, Kev. Make her moan more."

He pumped faster and as his rhythm increased she felt him getting close, his cock hardening even more and she groaned louder. Then he was pulling out and starting to slide it into her ass, banging that the way he had banged her pussy.

"Close," he breathed out, "not gonna last, it's super-tight and…" with a groan and a last thrust he came in her ass.

As his hips fell away and his cock popped out of her hole, her legs began to tremble in exhausted pleasure, the feeling of the cum slipping out of all her holes a tactile sensation of the erotic thrill of being banged in a virgin hole that throbbed with pleasure.

"I'm having a piece of that ass," Ryan said, his eyes smoldering with desire to penetrate the one hole he hadn't.

Ryan gripped her upper arms, turned her around and laid down on the desk with her back on his chest, his erection digging into her, as she squirmed on top of him, he started to wedge his cock into her ass and she fought him. That, of course, just pushed her ass on his shaft until it had filled her hole to bursting. She was pinned on top of him by his huge cock and it made her pussy throb to be filled, opening and closing with her need.

With her legs spread and her ass filled, Jason loomed over the top of her, "I'm going to fuck your snatch now that he's in your ass," as he slid his cock into her pussy, cum dripping out of both holes, pushed out as the cocks plunged in and out of both holes.

Just as she wanted to ask them to stop, a delicious friction began. Jason's groin pressed against her clit as Ryan's balls squeezed against her pussy. That made the pressure grow between her legs again, heat flooded her extremities and climbed her body, exploding in her pussy, squeezing both mens' cocks as they came together. Jason's head was thrown back and Ryan's rapped the wood of the desk as he thrust it back, her body an erotic tether holding the men together inside her, as her body stiffened between the men and her breathing became ragged as she screamed her orgasm into the still air of her classroom.

They lay there inside her for a moment then gradually, Jason loosened his hold, slipping out of her well-used part. Ryan sat up, still inside her and bodily picked her up, carefully setting her beside him.

And with a slow, long kiss he said, "Now that's a lesson we won't forget."

The Dara Nichols Series, 1-8 is available in paperback-

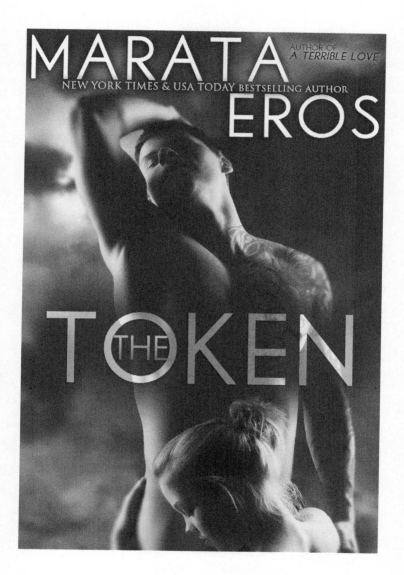

MARATA
AUTHOR OF
A TERRIBLE LOVE

NEW YORK TIMES & USA TODAY BESTSELLING AUTHOR

EROS

THE TOKEN

A dark romantic suspense

THE TOKEN-*chapter one*

Volume One

Copyright © 2013 Marata Eros

DEDICATION:

Autumn Tackett- Davis
Thank you so much~

"Love sears the heart immortal
The embers burnt down to the token which remains...."

PROLOGUE

"You're dying," Dr. Matthews says.

Two words.

Final.

Complete.

Desolate.

I feel my fingers clench the armrests of the chair underneath me, but the rest of my body remains numb.

If his words aren't enough to convince me, I see my silence is a prevailing annoyance in his day.

Dr. Matthews walks stiffly, making his way to the softly glowing X-ray reader.

I flinch when he slaps the photo of the soft tissue of my brain against the magnetic tabs of the lit surface.

The light glows around the tumor, immortalizing the end of my life like an emblazoned tool of disregard.

Just the facts, ma'am.

I sway as I stand, gripping the solid oak of his desk. It's very large, an anchor in the middle of his prestigious office full of the affectations of his career.

MARATA EROS

I walk toward Matthews. His hard face is edged by what might be sympathy. After all, it's not every day he tells a twenty-two-year-old woman she's got moments to live.

Actually, I do have time—months.

It's just not enough.

I look at the mess that's my brain, at the damning half a golf ball buried in a spot that will make me a vegetable if they operate. My eyes slide to the name at the bottom. For a split second, I hope to see another name there. But my own greets me.

Mitchell, Faren.

I back up and Matthews reaches to steady me.

But it's too late.

I spin and run out of his office as his voice calls after me. The corners of my coat sail behind me as I slap the metal hospital door open and take the cement steps two at a time.

I see my car parked across the street and race to it. My escape, my despair, is a thundering initiative I can't deny.

I miss the hit as if it happens to someone else. Only the noise permeates my senses as light flashes in my peripheral vision, mirrors against sunlight. I tumble in a slow spin of limbs. My body heaves and rolls, hitting the asphalt with a breath-stealing slap.

I lie against the rough black road. My lungs beg for air, burning for oxygen, and finally I take a sucking inhale that tears through my lungs.

The wet road feels cool against my face as I watch someone come into my line of sight. My body burns and my head aches. My arm is a slim exclamation point from my body, my fingers twitching. I can't make them stop. I can't make anything stop.

Powerless.

The doctor is too late with his condemning words. I've already died. I know this because the man who approaches is an angel. A helmet comes off hair so deep auburn it's a low-burning lick of flame. He swims toward me like a mirage, walking in a surreal slow motion. I blink, and my vision blurs. I try to raise my arm to wipe my eyes and whimper when it disobeys my command.

My angel crouches down, his eyes a deep brown, belying the dark bronze of his hair. "Shhh…I got you." His voice is a deep melody.

I sigh. Safe.

I try to focus on him but the helmet he parks next to his boots becomes three as my vision triples.

There's a scuffle and I try to move to see what all the commotion's about. The angel wraps his warm large hand around my smaller one and smiles. "It's going to be okay."

That's when I know I'm not in heaven.

That's what people say when nothing is okay.

1

One month prior

I flex my hand, grab my isometric handgrip, and do my hundred reps. So fun—a little like flossing my teeth. I put on the kettle with my good hand and turn the burner on high.

Flex, squeeze, release, flex again.

I get to a hundred and switch hands. As I go through my daily ritual, I flip open my Mac and browse my emails.

Faren, can you cover my shift? Faren, can you come in a half hour early? Faren, can you bring the main dish for the office pot luck?

Delete, delete, delete.

I'll say yes because it's hard for me to say no. Tough lessons in life have taught me that.

I put my handgrip on the corner of the end table, glancing at my left pinky and frowning. It's almost straight. Almost. No one can tell unless they're looking for it. No one ever looks that hard. Humanity glosses over shit.

I leave my laptop open and walk back to the stove. Depression-era jadeite salt and pepper shakers stand dead in the middle of a 1950s pink stove. The combo reminds me of an Easter egg. The kettle insists it's ready, bleating like a sheep. I lift it carefully, deliberately, using all the muscles of my hands as I've been taught.

As I teach others to do.

I pour the hot water over the tea bag and sigh, forcing my bad hand to thread through the loop of the tea cup handle. My dexterity is returning. I've pushed myself so hard that my hand rebels, willfully abandoning its hold on the cup.

The porcelain shatters, and shards fly on the wood floor of my tiny apartment above the main street where I live in deep anonymity. The pieces splinter in all directions, and I sigh. I want to chop off my hand.

I want to cradle it against my chest because it still works. Just not perfectly.

Like my life.

⌒

"Another headache?" Sue asks.

I nod, my hands falling away from my temples as I reach for my patient folder. I grip it with both hands and scan who's up first.

Bryce Collins. Pain. In. My. Ass.

I grin. I love the tough nuts to crack. They make it all worth it. I stride to my torture chamber, pushing the door open with my hip and search through the sea of work out equipment and hand held physical therapy implements to meet the sullen gaze of a seventeen-year old athletic prodigy.

A prodigy with a chip on his shoulder so wide I could drive a truck through it. Well I have my own dings and dents. We can compare later.

Right now, it's all about the work.

"Hi, Bryce."

He mumbles a reply as I hand him the first merciless task. The huge rubber band fits around the pole in the center of the room. Mirrors line the wall and toss back our struggles.

And our triumphs.

I watch as he half-heartedly goes through the motions of his straight leg kicks. When he reaches twenty I scoop my hand down and latch onto his hamstring and he groans at my touch. "Bend your knee a little," he does while giving me a look that could kill. I stare neutrally back until his gaze drops and he finally digs in.

An hour later, shaking and sweating, Bryce's huge and muscled body lumbers outside my door. He pauses as he opens it, looking at me with pissed off brown eyes.

"I hate you, Miss Mitchell," he says and means it.

I smile back. I totally get it. Bryce needs to hate me to get better. It beats hating himself. I nod. "I know."

He walks out, and I run my finger down the patient appointments for the day. Kiki makes her loud entrance, and my lips twist. She balances chai tea in both hands, staggering in too-tall heels that sink into the nearly bald carpet.

"Gawd!" she huffs as she winds her way through the ellipticals, weight machines, and treadmills. She leans against the walking bars that run like railroad tracks for those with dual injuries. Like both legs not working.

I swallow and force my smile back in place.

"Take your tea, you ungrateful bitch," she squeals, handing me my tea.

I blow on it. A touch of honey and ginger rise through the vapor, and I grin over the rim of the cup as I sip through the little slot.

"So?" I ask in a purr.

Kiki is pure drama. It's only Monday, so we have the entire week to build up to a crescendo. Mondays are usually sedate, so I brace myself. I have thirty minutes until my next client arrives to be tortured into wellness. Kiki smirks, sets down her tea, and moves to the pole. I give a furtive glance around the gym, hoping no one comes in.

"Got a..." She wraps around the pole and slides down it seductively, letting her butt cheeks split as she wiggles and bounces at the bottom. She springs up, the front of her hoohah a hairsbreadth from the cool metal. "Ginormous tip this weekend from a richie!"

She thrusts forward, wrapping one slender leg around the pole, and I groan. She does a little mock-hump against it and grins at me.

Kiki is so inappropriate I could die. But she's my drug and I'm hers. We fit together because we're so different.

She's an exotic dancer who's also a senior at Northwestern State.

She makes great money, and she also does serious gym time, packing in an hour six days a week. It's important to not look too striated, Kiki claims. No "guy-look." Just tits, ass, and curves with definition. I designed the workout for her because I'm intimately familiar with the human body. I didn't set out to be, but life had other plans.

The sins of the past become the direction of our future.

Kiki pouts, leaves the pole, and saunters toward me. "You're no fun."

I roll my eyes. "Okay...I know I've got to ask the burning question or we'll get nowhere."

She perks up. "You got it, sister."

"Who was it?"

Kiki always takes stock of clients. Men think they know so much, but women could rule the world if we came together. I sigh. Kiki notices regulars, high tippers, newcomers and flags the creeps. She's scary uncanny. I came to watch a set at the prestigious strip club, Black Rose, and went away shocked.

Shocked by the clientele, shocked that Kiki could dance that well for such a short time, and shocked by the moolah.

"The owner," Kiki whispers as if we have a secret.

I shrug. "So?"

"It's Jared-effing-McKenna, baby!" Kiki is offended by my deliberate ignorance. Her brows rise to her hairline, and her dark eyes are wide with clear disdain.

Mine are steady with indifference.

MARATA EROS

The wheels of my memory spin. *Oh yes.* Jared McKenna. *The* Jared McKenna. Greek god. Adonis incarnate. Hercules. Playboy, womanizer, money mogul.

I slowly nod. Let's add "strip club owner" to the repertoire. I remember the detail of *why* he has so much money and want to forget as soon as I do.

Kiki pouts and tears off the lid of her tea. "Anywho...he was with someone, and his pal tipped me big time." She sips her cooling tea, gazing at me with "cat that ate the canary" eyes.

"Okay, the foreplay is killing me. How much?" I take a small slurp of tea, and she tells me. The tea sprays out of my mouth, and Kiki grins at my klutzy-ass move.

"Five hundred dollars!?" I choke some more, and tea dribbles down my chin.

"It's okay, baby...it *is* a mind-blower. I mean," her hands go to her ample chest in patent disbelief, "my nipples got hard and he didn't even touch me," she says sincerely and I burst out laughing. My headache is gone for the moment, my Monday morning lethargy lifting.

Five hundred bucks is an assload of cash, especially for one night of dancing half naked. It's more than I take home every week. *Just one tip.* My schooling is done, my career path set partly because of circumstance. Kiki is high on drama, but doesn't always say things without a purpose and I narrow my eyes at her.

"Spill it," I demand.

Kiki's lips twitch and she chucks her empty cup in the trash. "This type of gig could be the thing to get you out of that dump in downtown."

I scowl. I like my downtown dump.

"Faren!" she wails.

I shush her before Sue comes in thinking someone died. Of course, with all the sounds of torment she's heard since I began working here last year, nothing should faze her.

Kiki relents and switches to a softer tone. "You could own something. Something nice."

I know this. I've been to her condo overlooking Pike Place and Puget Sound. Her view of downtown is magnificent. And expensive. It had to set her back five hundred K. I rent my death trap for nine hundred per month, and it's a studio in one of the tortuously small cobblestone-lined alleys of Seattle. At least it's on the fifth floor. The stairs are murder, but if I want two windows that actually face outside, that's what I can afford. Sometimes the freight elevator works; otherwise, it's exercise. The location allows me to walk to my upper-scale rehabilitation clinic. No need to use my beater car. That much.

"You don't have to give this up," Kiki says quietly. She knows I won't budge on that, and she of all people knows why.

Rehab's not a well-paying profession. But there's more than money, sometimes the soul needs edification.

I look at what Kiki has and what I don't. I shove those thoughts away. She's my best friend. She's seen me through everything. Dark shadows press in, and my headache returns with a throbbing vengeance.

Kiki frowns. "Another headache?"

"Yeah."

"I don't want to argue, Faren. You've got to know that." Her root beer eyes peg me to the spot. The sweep of her dark hair lays like chocolate silk past her full breasts. "But with your looks"—she throws her manicured hands in the air—"you could shake your booty a little and work a side job. Get a place in your same area…you could own something."

It's an old argument. Her penthouse is nearly paid for while mine's a rental with a landlord that cares more about the rent than maintenance.

Her eyes swim with knowledge, and I set down my tea. It's too cold to drink anyway. Her words put the last nail in the coffin of my resistance. "Something secure," she adds in a whisper and I let her hug me. I cling to her and try to believe my financial troubles and dark secret can be erased by taking off my clothes for strangers

Kiki loves me more than I love myself.

She loves me enough for us both.

⟋⟍

Sue glances up when I click off the light off. The sky is darkening as I slide my last patient folder through the glass partition. She has that look in her eyes and pushes a business card through the slot.

It bears a doctor's name: Dr. Clive Matthews.

I give Sue a sharp look, and she shrugs, giving my hand a maternal pat. My eyes burn with tears from the spontaneous gesture.

Sue notices my emotional struggle and ignores it. "He got rid of my migraines. Miracle worker, I say." She nods and glances at the card significantly.

I notice the appointment time and sigh.

Sue doesn't drop her gaze. "How much longer are you going to struggle through those bone crushers?"

I don't answer, and she nods in her knowing way. "That's what I thought, Miss Mitchell. You'd have just come in suffering worse than your own patients."

Sue's right. She knows it, and I do too.

I take the card and stuff it in the pocket of my smock, Dr. Seuss cats cover it in a smear of red and blue.

"Thanks," I say grudgingly while I grab my coat.

"Welcome," she shoots back in triumph as I hear the door whisper closed behind me.

I look at the card again as the cars, people, and city noise encapsulate me in the comforting rhythm of downtown. The smell of fish, food, and sea mingle, and I begin the short trek to the dank alley with the entrance to my apartment.

I have two weeks to prepare myself to go back into a hospital. I hate hospitals. They're all about death.

The thought of returning is almost enough to get a proper panic attack going.

Almost.

⌒

Love the preview? The Token series, 1-9 is available in paperback~

NEW YORK TIMES BESTSELLING AUTHOR
TAMARA ROSE BLODGETT

BLOOD
Singers
A BLOOD NOVEL

A dark paranormal vampire fantasy

BLOOD SINGERS- *bonus excerpt*

Book One: The Blood Series

Copyright © 2007-2012 Tamara Rose Blodgett

http://tamararoseblodgett.blogspot.com/

Edited by Stephanie T. Lott

Cover Design: Claudia McKinney
Photographs: DepositPhotos
Photography: Oleg Gekman

DEDICATION:

The girls that keep me Sane on Shelfari (and otherwise):
Beth and Dianne
I love you guys~

Once they had eliminated the impossible, whatever remained, however improbable, must be the truth.

~Sherlock Holmes

PROLOGUE

Julia pressed her nose to the glass, the trees a sea of green as they rushed outside her window, her momma and daddy's voices a low and pleasant drone from the front seat.

She hated the belt, it pressed across her neck in an uncomfortable place, itchy and suffocating.

"Momma," Julia whined plaintively.

Her mother's chocolate eyes appeared over the front seat, such a contrast to the auburn hair held in her customary pony tail.

"What is it?"

Julia worked her small finger under the belt and said, "I hate, HATE this stupid strap! I want to take it off!" Julia crossed her arms, huffing.

Momma sighed, unlatching her belt as she turned in the front seat to adjust the neck restraint portion of Julia's seatbelt. As Momma got nearer Julia smelled the special perfume that she wore. At once Momma's scent assaulted her where it intimately combined with the perfume she always wore.

Daddy said from the front, "Amber, sit back down. The belt's latched, she's just going to have to deal with it for another ten minutes."

Julia's eyes narrowed to slits. Daddy was so stubborn. *His* belt didn't bite into *his* neck! 'Cuz he was a Big Man! Ugh...Julia fumed.

Momma smiled and began to turn and Julia saw Daddy's face in profile, watching to make sure she sat down safely.

He only took his eyes off the road for a moment.

It was enough.

Julia saw twin beads of light bear down on their car as an impossibly large grill came to eat them, the chrome winking in the late afternoon light.

Daddy made a correction to the right but that threw Momma on top of him, imprisoning their bodies in a macabre dance, the steering wheel sandwiching them together.

As if in slow motion Julia saw her mother's face as Amber looked at her father.

The knowledge of their impending death appeared on their faces like an unspoken promise.

Julia screamed as the truck slammed into the car and the belt that she hated so much whipped against her neck and slammed her against the back seat with such force that the breath left her small body.

She watched her parents crushed together in a final embrace.

The metal colliding was an earthquake in her ears and something wet and warm hit her face. She opened her eyes and her parents were…everywhere, their blood like a blanket that coated her face and hair.

Her brain howled, refusing to accept what was happening. Her vision clouded. Her neck and head throbbed and her lungs were a burning inferno with the need to scream.

The last thing she remembered was her mother's hair entwined in the steering wheel like so much spun copper.

1

Ten Years Later

Julia stuffed her wool cap down more firmly on her head and waded through the icy puddles on the way to her 1977 Chevy Blazer. Fall had edged into early winter and the dampness of the rain had solidified into a dangerous sheet of ice.

Julia had known better and instead of wearing the latest Ugg fashion boots she'd slogged on her XtraTufs. They had an unparalleled ugliness but did the job. She might keep her ass in the air instead of pegged on an ice puddle by wearing her trusty boots. She threw her backpack over one shoulder and balanced a steaming cup of coffee in the other hand. She'd lied through her teeth about the contents to Aunt Lily, who seemed to think caffeine was the devil's drink. Julia smiled at that. She thought she was done growing and besides, coffee was a mainstay of Alaskan existence. She shuffled to the driver's side and gripped the handle. Then her feet lost some of their purchase and she slid to the right, her coffee sloshing out of the slit on the travel mug.

"Shit!" Julia said, as a couple of hot drops landed on her wrist, scalding her.

Grappling with the handle she jerked the door open and threw her palm on the driver's seat, steadying herself until she could heave her backpack inside.

But her breath stilled in her lungs when she saw what waited for her.

A single rose, its tremulous form in a beautiful, ethereal tangerine color lay inches from where her reddened and chapped hand had slapped down.

She'd almost destroyed it while saving her sliding butt from falling.

A smile stole over her face and she carefully put her travel mug in the cup holder between the seats and picked up the flower.

No note.

But she knew who had laid it there.

Her fiancé, Jason. Actually, it was a secret. Lily would have ten different kinds of cows if she knew how serious they were.

She looked around, her breath coming in white puffs in the crisp air. The snow having not committed itself to falling yet, the promise still hung there in the air. It would be like him, Julia thought, to pop up and grab her from behind, twirling her around just as she discovered his present.

But he wasn't there.

Huh, she turned the keys and jacked up the heat all the way. Five minutes and she'd hit the road, head to Homer

High. She was spoiled. Usually Jason picked her up but today she had to head over to the DMV and get a stupid emissions test. It was amazing they even allowed her to drive her gas-guzzling truck. She sighed. Soon, she'd be with Jason.

school

Julia tore off her multi-colored itchy hat as she waltzed into the school. The familiar smell of kids, books, lunch and all the other school fragrances wafting across the air, the chill of late fall left outside the doors.

She fluffed her champagne-colored hair, hoping to eradicate the hat head she'd tagged herself with on the way over.

"Hey, bestie!" Cynthia cried.

Julia laughed, like she hadn't just spent all day and a night last weekend with Cyn? She acted like they'd been separated for months.

"Hey Cyn," Julia said slowing, letting her catch up.

As usual, Cyn was dressed to the nines. High heels, ridiculously tight-ass pants and the latest, off-the-shoulder top with a crazy zebra pattern. It made Julia dizzy looking at it.

"What?" Cynthia looked at Julia's face.

"Your top, it's like some kind of optical illusion or something."

"I know, right? It's hot-hot-hot," she snapped her fingers after each word for emphasis. Julia rolled her eyes, there was no cure for her Fashion Awareness.

Julia considered herself Fashion Challenged. Yessiree. Irrefutably. Getting everything to match and be comfortable was of utmost importance.

Of course, once Julia mentioned Cyn's shirt, then she was honor bound to give Julia the once-over. Scanned from the top of her head she had almost escaped the wrath when Cynthia's gaze landed like a lead weight on her boots.

"Argh!" she shrieked in horror. "You wore your Tufs to school again! And don't give me any of that horse shit about how we're seniors and absolved of everything," she rolled her eyes dramatically, "fashion is the exception. And those," she waggled her fingers at Julia's offending footwear, "are for...for..."

"Gardening only," Jason interjected smoothly, his arm sliding around Julia's waist. He'd heard the XtraTufs speech before.

"Don't you defend her either!" Cynthia lambasted him and Jason, all mock innocence said, "Who me?" his hand to his chest.

Cynthia's eyes narrowed to slits. "You're no help, Jason Caldwell, she could wear a shapeless sack over her whole body and you'd still think she was gorgeous."

"Guilty," he said, his forehead dipping to peck Julia's head, still fuzzy from the hat.

Julia leaned back against his chest, her head tucking comfortably underneath his chin and sighed. This is where she'd wanted to be from the moment she opened her eyes. Against him, soaking up his warmth. Letting it seep into her bones and chase the coldness of the morning away.

Cyn snapped her fingers in front of Julia's face, "snap out of it Jules!"

Jason laughed, Julia was known to mentally wander. It was becoming an annoying theme lately.

"What? Cranky witch!" Julia teased, taking a swipe at Cyn with her woolen hat.

She ducked smoothly, accustomed to Julia's abuse. "Okay…so, did you get that English paper done we started on Friday?"

Julia dug around in her backpack until she found a crumpled piece of paper at the bottom and turning, she slapped it against her locker, smoothing it with her other hand. Jason's big hand was a warm presence on her shoulder, kneading it softly.

"Are you kidding? Terrell will never accept that mess," Cynthia said, throwing out one hip and putting a hand on the jutting point.

Julia shrugged a shoulder. "It's a rough draft. Besides, keeping the standard low like I do assures me gravy when I turn something in."

Julia smiled at her awesome logic. School just didn't appeal. It was something she survived until she could graduate. It was Jason that was going to University of Alaska Anchorage. He was set with a full ride.

Mr. Basketball. Julia turned to look at him and wondered for the millionth time why he'd want her. He was so gorgeous and she was so…her. It didn't matter that Cyn thought she was pretty. Whatever. Cyn was her BFF, that's what they do, cheerlead.

Julia still didn't have A Plan. She knew she couldn't wait to get out of Aunt Lily's place and begin a life with Jason.

Cynthia gave an elaborate roll of her eyes and caved, saying, "You can try all your down home weasel-like charm on Terrell while Jason and I turn in real papers. Unwrinkled papers." She cocked her brows up to her hairline and looping her arm through Julia's, she dragged her to block one.

The Dreaded Language Arts. Everyone knew there was nothing artful about it. Jason laughed as they trudged to class, Julia's arms linked with theirs.

Love Blood? **BLOOD SINGERS** *is available in paperback-*

ACKNOWLEDGMENTS

I began The Druid Series with the encouragement of my husband and continued because of you, my Reader. Your faithfulness through comments, suggestions, spreading the word and ultimately purchasing my work with your hard-earned money gave me the incentive, means and inspiration to continue.

There are no words that are sufficiently adequate to express my thankfulness for your support. But know this: TDS novellas continued past HARVEST only because of you.

I truly feel connected to my readers. It is obvious to me, but I'll say the words anyway for clarity: a written work is just words on pages if they are not read by my readers. As I write this I get a lump in my throat; your enjoyment of my work affects me that deeply.

You guys are the greatest, each and every one of ya~
Marata xo

Dear Ones:

You, my reader.
My husband, who is my biggest fan.
Cameren, without whom, there would be no books.

Special Thanks:

Hazel Novak., my copy editor. Thank you readers, by supporting my work you've provided me with the means to give you cleaner copy.
Lisa O., my proof reader.
Ange
Autumn
Beth Dean Hoover
Crystal
Rônin

More Books
by Marata Eros:

The Druid Series:
Reapers
Bled
Harvest
Sow
Seed
Plow
Thresher
Exotic
The Druid Breeders
Baird

The Siren Series:
Ember
Constantine
Brandon (available for paperback pre-order)

The Demon Series:
Brolach

The Token Serial:
The Token
The Token 2
The Token 3
The Token 4
The Token 5

The Token 6
The Token 7: Thorn
The Token 8: Kiki (available for paperback pre-order)
*The Token 9: Chet Sinclair (*available for paperback
pre-order)

Dark Romantic Suspense:
A Terrible Love
A Brutal Tenderness
The Darkest Joy
In Broken Love- 2015

The Dara Nichols Series, 1-8:
3500-5500 words each *(naughty & sexual, non-romantic
encounters)*

A Hard Lesson, where Dara Nichols gets "schooled" by
a few students…

To Protect and Service, Dara gets pulled over by the
cops and taken in hand…

The 13th Floor, Dara attends a professors' symposium
and things heat up in the elevator…

The Boardroom, Dara's sexual encounter with her students is discovered and she receives some much-deserved
discipline…

The Four Whoresmen, Dara takes a weekend getaway at
a remote ranch and gets man-handled…

The Masquerader's Balls, Dara and Zoe get nailed by a couple of masked men...

The Ball Player, Dara takes one for the team at the local gym...

The Cock Tale, Dara and Zoe teach university president Craig Taylor a lesson in discipline at his own party...

Disclaimer: The DNS titles are a completely different "flavor" from the work that you just enjoyed. These are explicit erotica centered around sexual, non-romantic encounters. These short stories are more sexual in nature, whereas the dark paranormal novellas are more sensual/romantic tension/erotic romance-driven.

The ZOE SCOTT Series:
Smoldering Wet
The Zoe Scott Series, 1-8 (available for paperback pre-order)

BLOG: marataeroseroticaauthor.blogspot.com

BOOKS WRITTEN UNDER MARATA'S REAL NAME, TAMARA ROSE BLODGETT:

BLOG: Tamara Rose Blodgett

The Death Series
(young/new adult dark paranormal dystopian fantasy):

Death Whispers
Death Speaks
Death Inception
Death Screams
Death Weeps
Unrequited Death
The Death Bundle, books 1-3
For the Love of Death

The Savage Series
(new adult dark post-apocalyptic steampunk paranormal romance):

The Pearl Savage
The Savage Blood
The Savage Principle
The Savage Vengeance
The Savage Protector

The Savage Dream (available for paperback pre-order)
Savage Bundle, Books 1-3

The Blood Series
(new adult dark supernatural fantasy and paranormal romance):

Blood Singers
Blood Song
Blood Chosen
Blood Reign

*

The Reflection Series

(adult dark paranormal dystopian fantasy):

The Reflective (The Reflection Series, #1)

Marata Eros (the pen name for Tamara Rose Blodgett), is the author of over forty titles, including her NEW YORK TIMES and USA TODAY bestselling novel, *A Terrible Love*. Marata writes a variety of dark fiction in the genres of fantasy, science fiction, romance and erotica. She lives in South Dakota with her family and enjoys interacting with her readers.

Never miss a SPAM-FREE new release,
update or exclusive excerpt!
SUBSCRIBE: http://tinyurl.com/MarataErosNewsletter

Website: http://marataeroseroticaauthor.blogspot.com/

Twitter: https://twitter.com/MarataEros

Facbook: https://www.facbook.com/pages/
Marata-Eros/336334243087970

Goodreads: http://www.goodreads.com/author/
show/5052261.Marata_Eros

Pinterest: http://www.pinterest.com/marataeros/

Made in the USA
Monee, IL
28 December 2020

55635568R00194